PRAISE FOR MARTINE DESJARDINS

Maleficium

Winner 2013 Sunburst Award

Shortlisted 2010 Governor General's Literary Award (French Fiction)

Winner 2010 Prix Jacques-Brossard

Shortlisted 2010 Prix des libraires du Québec

2010 Prix des cinq continents de la Francophonie

"[Martine Desjardins] has dared to write a book unlike any other, dipping her pen in the ink of a bygone day, before nature and its mysteries had been deciphered; when desire loomed with dark and frightening power. The result is an extraordinary festival of the senses." —*Voir*

"Transports readers to new terrain altogether."—*Quill & Quire*

"Lust, greed, retribution, and shame – *Maleficium* reads like a flesh-bound catalogue of my favourite sins ... an intensely pleasurable work that builds, tale by exotic tale, to a dark climax. Forgive me, Father: I loved it." —Jenn Farrell

A Covenant of Salt

"Mining from the past, Desjardins extracts treasures without 'getting caught,' and surfaces like a breath of fresh air. *A Covenant of Salt* marries literary traditions in a sleek gothic ceremony, silvery salt sprinkled like confetti and the Saint Lawrence coursing through." —*Montreal Review of Books*

Also by

MARTINE DESJARDINS

and published by Talonbooks

All That Glitters

A Covenant of Salt

Fairy Ring

The Green Chamber

Maleficium

←MEDUSA→

A Novel

MARTINE DESJARDINS

Translated by Oana Avasilichioaei

TALONBOOKS

Talonbooks
9259 Shaughnessy Street, Vancouver, British Columbia, Canada v6p 6r4
talonbooks.com

Talonbooks is located on xʷməθkʷəy̓əm, Sḵwx̱wú7mesh, and səl̓ilwətaʔɬ Lands.

First printing: 2022

Typeset in Sabon
Printed and bound in Canada on 100% post-consumer recycled paper
Cover design and graphics by Ginger Sedlarova and Typesmith
Interior design by Typesmith
Inside cover images: *Sky* by Andrew Beatson, and *Lake* by Lachlan Ross

Talonbooks acknowledges the financial support of the Canada Council for the Arts, the Government of Canada through the Canada Book Fund, and the Province of British Columbia through the British Columbia Arts Council and the Book Publishing Tax Credit.

This work was originally published in French as *Méduse* by Les Éditions Alto, Québec City, Québec, in 2020. We acknowledge the financial support of the Government of Canada through the National Translation Program for Book Publishing, an initiative of the *Roadmap for Canada's Official Languages 2013–2018: Education, Immigration, Communities*, for our translation activities.

Library and Archives Canada Cataloguing in Publication

Title: Medusa : a novel / Martine Desjardins ; translated by Oana Avasilichioaei.
Other titles: Méduse. English
Names: Desjardins, Martine, 1957- author. | Avasilichioaei, Oana, translator.
Description: Translation of: Méduse.
Identifiers: Canadiana 20220238308 | ISBN 9781772013856 (softcover)
Classification: LCC PS8557.E78284 M4313 2022 | DDC C843/.54—dc23

for Antoine

I've never shed a tear in my entire life. Not out of sadness, anger, anguish, pain, let alone laughter or happiness. Not even the tiniest crocodile tear.

I'm not writing this to you so I can boast about having no feelings or being particularly stoic in the face of adversity. The explanation for my ocular dryness is more physiological in nature: I suffer from congenital atrophy of the lacrimal glands, which produce just enough liquid to moisten my conjunctivae, but not enough to form tears. Even dust, cold air, smoke, peeled onions, and tear gas leave my eyes more desiccated than a dried-up well. I'll never feel the consolation of snivelling about my sad fate, bawling like a cow when I stub my toe against the furniture, inundating my cheeks after being humiliated, or wringing my handkerchief over some tear-jerker.

The other night, when you pressed me to tell you why I'm so ashamed of my eyes, this lacrimal deficiency is the first thing that came to mind. Of all the unnatural defects that plague my Deformities, this has to be the lesser one, and yet I couldn't bring myself to admit it to you. I was left speechless, beak nailed shut by the hammer of my mortification, taken down a peg or two ... and the moment of truth turned into an aphonic, awkward silence.

Today, however, I'm not at all embarrassed to share this obscene detail of my ocular anatomy with you because the resin is numbing my natural modesty and stupefying my inhibitions: I've already chewed so much that my teeth are as black as Tahitian pearls.

Dazed, disoriented, slightly euphoric, I'm slumped in an armchair in the library, before a notebook laced by the shadows of lamps, preparing to put my reckless pen to paper and recount to you the full story of my abjection. My hand wanders and my writing turns in circles, but I'm staying the course: the resin clarifies my thoughts and concises my emotions; it curtails regrets and obliterates remorse. Don't worry! I'm not about to wallow in piteous outpouring: I can assure you that no tear will ever blur the ink of this pithy confession.

I think I've always known that I had Monstrosities instead of eyes. But I became fully aware of it one evening when my mother put her hand over my eyelids before leaning over my bed to tuck me in.

From that moment on, I stopped struggling when she combed my hair in the morning. The task was arduous because I had thick, curly hair, unruly and tangled up in knots, of a scaly texture that irritated the fingers and resisted scissors. Somehow my mother would manage to brush my bangs forward, so that they completely hid my face, and take the opportunity to give me an affectionate warning:

"If you ever show your eyes, I'll have to sew your lids shut."

I had no reason to doubt her words: she was skilled with the needle, having herself embroidered with red or gold thread the academic logos adorning my father's socks. He was the proud rector of the university and never took off his academic gown and tasselled mortarboard except to go to sleep. He'd shut himself in his study as soon as he came home and, since I didn't take my meals with the rest of the family, I rarely found myself in his presence. Generally speaking, he was happy ignoring my existence; if he needed to discipline me, he'd always spank my backside because my frontal view was offensive to him.

My two sisters, older than me by a few years, had the bewitching peridot-green eyes of does and luxuriant hair that fell to their waists in silky, glossy curls. They were the pride and joy of our parents and begrudged me for marring, by my defective existence, the familial lustre they polished with such care. They would accuse me of having the evil eye and shut the door in my face if I was unfortunate enough to go near their bedroom.

Of course, I often wondered what was so repulsive about my Hideousnesses to incite such repugnance in my family. I imagined reptilian eyes with vertical pupils or bug eyes with iridescent facets, lumps of coal, glass marbles, octopus suckers, thorny globes, cysts engorged with blood, ulcerous pustules, teeming spiders, slimy oysters, lamprey mouths with murderous teeth ...

Do you understand now why I never had the curiosity to see myself in the mirror? I would've rather been enucleated than know the true face of my ugliness. I would turn away from all transparent surfaces – windows, glasses, crystal vases, framed prints, ornamental display cases. I would wash without lifting my face to the mirror hanging above the sink, bathe with my head held high in the air to avoid my image in the water's surface. I lived in constant fear of catching my reflection in the blade of a knife or the hollow of a spoon. I felt safe only in the dark, once I could close my lids at last.

No, I didn't need a mirror to know that I was the ugliest person in the world. Bearing the burden of my Repellencies and being condemned to live the life of an outcast was enough.

I learned to walk with my back stooped, head bent beneath the yoke of opprobrium, shoulders hunched forward, chin glued to sternum, lids half-closed, using my hands to blindly guide me, since I could barely see two feet in front of me. I must've cut a sad figure, as my dear sisters would make fun of me constantly and compare me, depending on their mood, to a mop, a lampshade, or a sheepdog.

As I never dared to raise my head and look directly at my family members, I only knew their faces from the photographs in an album that didn't include me. However, I remember my father's feet, vainly garbed in embroidered socks; those of my mother, toes tightly squeezed in pointy heels; and those of my sisters, shod in satin slippers. And, of course, my own, laced up in a used pair of boots, humbly pigeon-toed. I also remember my sagging socks, the torn hem of my sisters' hand-me-down dresses, my nails bitten to the quick, the chipped edges of my plate, the strips of paper I chewed in secret.

With my neck going completely stiff, for hours I'd follow the haunting progress of a ray of sunlight across the room, observe the spontaneous formation of dust bunnies by the baseboards, contemplate the invariable geometry of shadows created by lamplight.

I'm afraid my memories of the family home are rather lowbrow. I could draw from memory the patterns of the parquet, the carpets and doormats, the legs of the furniture, the electrical sockets, the doorstops, the kitchen tiles, the mosaic in the bathroom, the paper baskets, the andirons in the fireplace ...

Behind the bushy bower of my mop of hair, I amused myself building castles in the air, a pastime at which I became exceptionally seasoned. All I had to do was stare at some pattern on the floor to make my sight go fuzzy and lose myself in a heady blur. In a short time, the parquet would start to undulate, the medallions of the carpet would become three-dimensional, the white tiles in the bathroom would pastel in pinks, blues, and purples ... With my sight cocooned in hypnotic emptiness, I would remain suspended in a stupor from which I never wanted to emerge.

I feasted on these ocular trances as though on exquisite forbidden fruit. Yet, as you know, this proved to be only a small taste of the vast sensorial register of my Anomalies.

My parents did me the great favour of not sending me to school, where I would've been the target of mischievous children. My mother took charge of my education – turning her back to me and discharging her duty in a very rudimentary fashion. I learned to read with a dog-eared alphabet primer. I still count on my fingers. You can see for yourself just how childish my handwriting is.

I certainly would've remained in abysmal ignorance if it wasn't for the instant attraction that the printed word inspired in my Infirmities. My sight magnetized against my will, I felt compelled to decipher, compulsively and indiscriminately, everything that fell into my hands: the label on a dress, the directions on a bottle of cough syrup, the signature at the bottom of a painting, the stock-market numbers in a newspaper, and the academic journals to which my father subscribed – even if I didn't understand all that much.

For me, books quickly became a screen behind which I could hide, and I got into the habit of always having one in front of my face. At first more laboriously, then with more ease, I burned through the textbooks my sisters discarded and the travel literature my mother loved. I soon had to supply myself from my father's library, which was as vast as it was varied.

Stretched out on the carpet on my stomach, nose sunk into the pages of the encyclopedia, I formed an idea of the world that was forbidden to me. I could never get tired of studying faces in illustrated books, examining the eyes all the more voraciously because my own Abysmalities were shielded from their looks.

In novels, I especially appreciated the character descriptions, even though certain passages remained as indecipherable as cryptograms. How could I have been able to distinguish between having steely or velvety eyes, being wide-eyed and giving someone the eye, between imploring, ingenuous, or provocative looks, friendly winks and murderous glares?

My reading wasn't always appropriate for a young girl's innocent mind, but there was no authority to censure my choices. As long as my Atrocities remained shut away in a book, my parents paid me no attention.

My father had a well-established reputation in the city, and he cared about it as if it was the apple of his eye. It goes without saying that he would never have compromised it by dragging me around like some kind of circus freak. When the members of my family would leave arm in arm for their Sunday outing, I'd be left behind, alone, and would kill time by moping in the pages of a book.

Upon their return, my sisters would hasten to humiliate me by recounting the minutiae of all they had seen: the changing of the guard in front of the citadel, the lighting of the oil lamps in the cathedral, the recital of a concert band on the château terrace, the arrival of ships in the harbour, the parade of animals at the zoo, the house of mirrors on the exhibition grounds, the performance of acrobats in front of the coliseum ...

"And how did you spend your wonderful day?" they'd ask me in a sarcastic tone.

One fall afternoon, they came home from their outing nudging and elbowing each other like they shared a big secret. Our parents had taken them to the new aquarium, and they described all the different galleries to me.

In the fresh water gallery, where the dull fish of our lakes and rivers swam, they had definitely preferred the exterior tank, where trained sea lions balanced balls on their noses. Yet it was the salt water gallery that had the biggest surprise in store for them. Amid the sea anemones, starfish, and other marine creatures, my sisters had stopped in front of the medusae, struck by their resemblance to me.

"They look like your twin sisters!" they insisted. "Your head is bell-shaped, your hair is made of tentacles, and your eyes are gonads! You should be in an aquarium!"

They pointed at me, bursting with laughter, and started chanting a refrain that grated my eardrums:

"Medusa! Medusa! Medusa!"

For me, this word instantly embodied all the aspects of my ugliness, and I understood it as the worst kind of insult. To my great annoyance, it quickly supplanted all other nicknames and has stuck to me for so long now that I've forgotten my actual name.

Even so, I should consider myself lucky: my sisters could've decided to call me Mop or Sheepdog.

Don't think, though, that I was confined to the house. With hygienic diligence, my mother granted me the privilege of going out as soon as a storm or downpour hit the city. She figured, quite rightly, that I'd basically go unnoticed in the harsh weather.

"Go on, get out of here!" she'd say, chasing me away with her hand as soon as I poked my nose outside. "Don't stay in front of the house like a halfwit. Go play somewhere else."

In summertime, I'd stay far away from the main boulevard with its gutters of shimmering puddles and keep to the back alley. Hood pulled over my Imperfections, hands stuffed in my pockets, I'd pace back and forth while the rain came down in buckets and the dogs in the neighbouring yards barked at my passing. They alone kept me company. I had no friends, but I no longer had any hopes of having them, either.

In wintertime, my route was essentially the same. One day when it was freezing cold, I defied my mother's authority and remained on the front steps, back turned to the icy blast of winter, stamping my feet to warm up my numb toes. I faced the front-door knocker – an ornament I'd never dared to look at before, afraid of seeing my Grossnesses in its polished brass surface. But since it was covered in frost, it presented no danger in its marmoreal dullness. I lifted my hood and even plucked up the courage to part my frozen bangs and take a better look.

The knocker's ring was made of serpents whose intertwined heads radiated from the head of a terrifying Medusa, her gaping mouth frozen in pain like a mime mask. I examined her eyes and they looked back at me indulgently, not contorting with disgust. Though they were still and absent, they seemed warmer to me than my mother's eyes. I was transfixed and stayed there, unblinking, imagining them looking emotional, smiling, gazing fondly at my Indignities with maternal kindness. Medusified by this vision, I forgot about the cold.

I also forgot about the vulnerability of my position, and what was bound to happen, happened. The front door suddenly flew open, and I found myself face to face with the maid, who was just going out. I barely had time to notice that she was all bundled up in a Persian lamb hat and coat with the collar raised. She was startled to see me and, almost instantaneously, started shrieking like she was possessed.

I was so dismayed to have been taken by surprise in the most intimate part of my nakedness that I considered fleeing. But a desperate powerlessness nailed me to the spot: where could I have run with my Impurities? So I simply closed my lids, pulled down my bangs, and buried my face in the prickly wool of my mittens.

My mother arrived at that moment. The maid told her that she would never set foot in the house again and quit on the spot. I heard the door bang shut and my mother sigh, her chest sinking in. Inside my mittens, my hands started shaking.

I didn't know what punishment would be inflicted on me, but I imagined the worst. At the thought that my mother would make good on her threat and sew my lids shut, a buzzing started vibrating my eardrums, hot blood rushed to my cheeks, saliva flowed in acidic jets under my tongue. I could've easily gotten used to never seeing my kind again but would never have been able to stand being deprived of the only refuge that reading offered me. Allow me to be a bit dramatic here: I would have died.

"Your father will deal with you," my mother said. "In the meantime, go up to your room and don't come out until he calls for you."

Relieved to have escaped the needle and thread, I worried that I'd be sent to reform school, an orphanage, an asylum, or even prison, where my Infuriations would surely attract the spite of scores of strangers. I suffered in the throes of anguish while waiting to learn my punishment. My father, however, meant to prolong the torment: I had to wait a week before finally being summoned to his study.

Reclining in his armchair, arms crossed behind his head and legs outstretched on the desk blotter, my father was busy admiring the embroidery on his socks, shimmering in the bright light of the lamp. With a jerk of his leg, he indicated that I should stay by the door.

"You're leaving tonight, go pack your bags. I'll wait for you in the car."

He gave no further explanation, and I returned to my room completely bewildered. I had very few possessions – some clothes and toiletries – so it didn't take me long to pack. I was in such a state of shock at the thought of leaving my shelter that I forgot to bring my books.

Neither my mother nor my sisters came to bid me good riddance at the foot of the stairs. I was saved, at least, from this humiliation.

My father made me sit in the back of the car and adjusted the rear-view mirror to avoid seeing my reflection. He had replaced his mortarboard with a hat, and from the back he was unrecognizable. I didn't dare ask him where he was taking me.

It was my first trip in a car, and I felt nauseous; not to mention that my thighs were freezing on the leather seat. I looked out the window. Through the condensation, I could see nothing but darkness on a moonless night.

We left the city behind and drove, at first, on country roads, then through an interminable forest. Spiky, hostile fir trees passed by with relentless monotony in the white fog of the headlights. No dwellings for miles around, no sign of civilization. My father could've made me get out and left me by the roadside, to the mercy of the cold, hunger, and wild animals: no one would've ever found me again. I wouldn't be surprised if he fantasized about it.

At last, the car turned onto a private road that led to the edge of a stagnant lake whose surface swallowed the glimmers of twinkling stars. From this cauldron of desolation rose a sticky, motionless mist and the brackish stink of rotten vegetables that stuck in my throat and chilled me to the bone.

The only sign of life on the bank of this wild expanse of water was a large, black-granite building, consisting of a corps de logis flanked by two lateral wings whose gloomy, brutal silhouette rose against the surrounding woods; the dimly lit windows were as narrow as arrow slits. A little to the side stood a large, empty, wrought-iron aviary.

There was something so inhospitable about the place that my stomach was all tied up in knots. I summoned just enough courage to ask my father:

"What is this place?"

"An institute," he answered in a gravelly voice I'd never heard before. "This is where we lock up monsters like you."

The institute was bolted by such heavy double doors that it took four matrons to open the two studded halves. These guardians were built like log drivers and had huge watchdogs on leashes who barked furiously at me, foaming at the mouth. I didn't bat an eyelid: I was used to inspiring aversion in the canine species.

My father prodded me in the back to get me to advance, and I tripped over the threshold; the echo of my fall resonated in the empty, cavernous hall. That's how I made my entrance: on my knees – which didn't bode well for my already heavily wounded pride. The floor was cold and hard under my bruised kneecaps; it was made of black basalt and inlaid with a medallion of cast steel, in which, between two stylized branches of laurel, stood the word *Athenaeum*.

This name from antiquity gave me a glimmer of hope: in ancient Rome, the Athenaeum was an academy of high repute, where rhetoricians discussed literature and philosophy. If this institute was a similar place of learning, I'd surely receive a real education here that would assuage my unfortunate ignorance.

Before I could stand up, my father grabbed me by the nape and dragged me to the centre of the hall, where two feminine feet awaited us strapped in a pair of Greek sandals, over which draped a cloth of purple silk. The feet, with yellowish nails as sharp as talons, were so scrawny that the pointy nodules of the tarsi, metatarsi, and phalanges of the toes stuck out between the sandal straps.

"So this is the one you call Medusa?" asked the woman who, it turned out, was the headmistress of the institute. "Let's see these eyes that are supposed to be so hideous."

Without any other preamble, she grabbed my fore-lock and threw it back. Instinctively, my lids snapped shut and, as they were determined to remain closed, the headmistress forced them open with her claw-like nails. Despite my confusion, I wasn't able to avoid the sight before me.

The headmistress was very tall and just as bony as her feet. She was swathed in a toga, which was clasped over the shoulder, exposing the stringy tendons of her neck that spanned fanlike to her protruding collar-bones. On her gloved hand perched an owl whose golden-brown plumage shimmered in the torchlight. The raptor swung its head towards me and fixed its eyes on my ophidian tresses, snapping its beak and kneading its talons like a kitten at her mother's teat.

The headmistress's skull was completely bald, her eyebrows and eyelashes also absent: she suffered from a rare form of congenital alopecia that accentuated, if that was even possible, her skeletal frame. She had a waxy complexion and dark circles under her eyes. Her lips, blue-black and severely puckered, probably almost never smiled. They twisted into a fierce grimace, and then I saw that her teeth were also black. As for her eyes, they were, in that instant, white with disgust.

"What horrors of nature!" she hissed, pushing me away at arm's length. "Makes you want to gouge them out."

The owl chose this dramatic moment to hoot a lugu-brious dirge. My father's hand came down on my head, and he bent my neck with such force that my cervical vertebrae cracked like a lifting jack. I wished, there and then, that he'd press even harder so that I could sink into the basalt floor to hide my shame.

The headmistress regained her composure before lashing out, "It's true that the mission of this institute is to welcome young girls ostracized by society because of their physical imperfections. However, there are limits to our charity. I'm sorry, but it's out of the question to admit such a creature within these walls. She would spread terror among our protégées."

My father's feet, in their rubber overshoes, started stomping on the spot. With a pleading voice, he insisted, "Couldn't you find some small corner for her with the servants? Regardless of your conditions, as long as I'm rid of her."

The headmistress reflected from a moment, then answered in a less-than-encouraging tone, "The benefactors of the institute will decide. Follow me."

She wasn't very steady on her feet, and each step threatened to throw her off balance. Endeavouring to maintain a dignified gait despite her titubation, she solemnly led us into the boardroom.

What I first noticed were the glaring spots the lamps projected onto the billiard-green carpet, the scratches etched into the leather of the club chairs, the dust accumulated on the books in the mahogany bookcases. Then I saw thirteen pairs of feet in patent-leather shoes, some very small, others oversized, approaching with curiosity and tightening the circle around me as I advanced into the room. I was in the presence of the Athenaeum's benefactors.

The headmistress took the floor and explained the gravity of my condition to these gentlemen. She didn't mince words or shovel it in either, I assure you. I was grateful to the benefactors that they took the headmistress at her word and didn't ask to see my Mutantesses firsthand. They simply expressed their great disappointment to be losing a protégée but accepted a servant out of respect for my father.

Despite her reticence, the headmistress accepted their decision – although imposing certain conditions: "She must always work on her hands and knees, eyes glued to the floor. And she must always walk with her face turned to the wall. If she ever raises her eyes to anyone, she'll be punished. If she misbehaves three times, she'll be sent back without appeal."

Naturally, I was disappointed to once again be denied an education. But deep down, I wasn't angry at the turn of events, since I was sure that my new situation would offer me more freedom: even if I had to clean the floors, I could rummage around in the library as I pleased … and I'd have some blessed peace. Separated from the protégées, I'd be forgotten without much difficulty; I'd pass undetected through the most obscure corners of the institute. As proof, the benefactors were already losing interest in the trifling matter of my person, and some had started to walk away.

Without asking my opinion, my father promised that I would blindly submit, then turned to me moodily to admonish me, "Is that understood, Medusa?"

Enthusiastically, I answered without a moment's thought, "Don't worry about me. I'm ready to grovel to never have to go back home!"

Perhaps it was a bit brazen of me. Ungrateful and also vindictive. I knew the moment the words came out of my mouth that I'd soon regret them.

All around me the murmuring stopped, glasses were emptied, cigars were snuffed out, and the patent-leather shoes closed ranks once again. The headmistress addressed my father: "Medusa is now subject to the rules of the Athenaeum, and here such insolence, especially from a servant, does not go unpunished. You have the honour of exercising your paternal rights one last time!"

The benefactors clapped their hands like children before some unexpected entertainment. They cleared their throats and with the utmost gravity recited in chorus a pompous litany to the glory of the institute and in memory of its founder. While they shuffled from one leg to the other, stomping on the carpet and kicking their heels, I kept quiet, heart in turmoil, wondering in what kind of occult brotherhood I had landed.

Without any warning, my father caught me under a vigorous arm, and I found myself bent over with my head between my knees. Before I could understand what was happening, my skirt had been raised over my backside. I tried to wriggle myself free, but I was immobilized.

For my father, whose pride came from his position, my reply must've represented overwhelming humiliation. I had made him lose face in public, and he was not embarrassed to return the favour. He raised his arm, and the slaps of his ire started coming down. He didn't give me a spanking; he beat the shit out of me. He hit me with the flat of his hand, with a scathing resentment I was sure went all the way back to the day of my birth.

Meanwhile, the benefactors were encouraging him with shrieks of admiration, tittering with childish excitement, whispering in their neighbour's ear some remark that would make them snigger. Increasingly rowdy, they shifted from foot to foot, making the patent leather of their shoes creak, laughing their heads off.

I closed my eyes and waited for the insult to finish. I felt no pain. Only a warm tingling about which I was hardly in a position to complain: it was, after all, the only fatherly warmth I had ever received.

When exhaustion overcame him at last, my father was obliged to stop and let me go. I stood up and readjusted my skirt as if I was smoothing out the last remaining tatters of my modesty. As for him, his face was flushed and he was having difficulty catching his breath. Between two wheezing gasps, he downed a glass offered by a benefactor and refused the cigar held out by another. Excusing himself on account of the long drive back, he thanked the board members and bid them good night.

He should've just cut and run. But no. He had to take me aside, by the door, and give me one last piece of advice: "Now that your poor mother is at last unburdened from the weight of your responsibility, it would be best not to disturb her peace. Don't send us any news and don't expect to receive any from us."

Instead of an affectionate goodbye, I sighed in exasperation. Unfortunately, I sighed with a bit too much force, and my bangs went flying in the air, exposing my entire forehead. My hair stayed in place, sticking up like a tuft. So, for the first time in my life, I saw my father's face up close.

He had light hair, a rather long face, and a dimple on his chin. For the rest, I don't know what to tell you because at that moment, he was disfigured by the grimaces of a stroke. All colour had drained from his face. His lips went dry and white. Of his frozen features, only his eyes were still animated: they rolled in their orbits counter-clockwise. And in his panic-stricken look, you could see the indescribable terror of someone being struck by lightning.

My father fell backwards and collapsed on the carpet like a felled tree. At the instant he stopped breathing, his still eyes glazed over, yet without losing their crazed expression. The last heartbeat resonated in his rib cage with the finality of a rock hitting the bottom of a well.

One of the benefactors, apparently a doctor, rushed to his aid. He tried to reanimate him, took his pulse, but it quickly became clear that his efforts were in vain. He closed my father's eyes and pronounced him dead due to heart failure because of the physical effort he'd expended earlier.

I didn't pretend to be saddened by my progenitor's death: I was even less attached to him than to my mother. He didn't figure in any of my memories, other than by his disdainful distance, which I wouldn't miss. Otherwise, I knew so little about his life that it was impossible for me to measure its loss.

The circumstances of his death, however, shook me to the core – and not just because I'd seen it up close. I didn't believe a word of the doctor's assessment. I was sure that exhaustion had nothing to do with it. I alone knew what had killed my father: the horror of seeing my Devastations.

The west wing of the institute was reserved for the benefactors, while the protégées slept in the east wing, where the corridors were full of drafts that seeped between the seams of your clothes and chilled you to the bone. The room the headmistress assigned me was located right under the eaves, at the top of a spiral staircase. It was tiny and its roof so low that I almost hit my forehead as I went in. Its sole source of light came from a narrow garret window: suffice it to say that on this moonless night, it was sunk in darkness.

However, to my great surprise, I didn't need to stumble in blindly. Through some unknown organic transformation, my Unsightlinesses had just acquired the ability to pierce through darkness. They could now discern the palest reflections on objects, distinguishing volumes as accurately as in broad daylight. Like the headmistress's owl, I now had night vision.

Thus I was able to ascertain that the furniture in the room was austere. I set my suitcase on the iron bed and opened the wardrobe to hang up my clothes. I was assailed by a waft of naphthalene and a black beetle that flew out of the shadows, then crashed on the floor. The insect scared me with the unsightly buzzing of its elytra and the wriggling of its crooked legs. I shivered in disgust, but just as I was about to squash it, felt pity for its ugliness, so I grabbed it between my fingers and opened the garret window to set it free.

The opening was just big enough for me to squeeze my head through. I scanned the horizon and nothing escaped my night vision – not even the tip of the bell tower miles away. Limited since childhood by the narrowness of my myopic perspective, I would never have guessed that my gaze could have such a panoramic scope.

From above, the lake looked like an extinct volcanic crater. It was hemmed in on all sides by a wall of firs and smothered by the bare branches of alders and viburnums. Although the arctic weather was numbing enough to crack trees, the water was barely frozen: the frazil on the surface was suspended in a grey and gelatinous sludge, with regular undulations like the respiration of someone sleeping.

My rapacious gaze pierced the rough layer of ice and I saw, through the nets of tentacular grasses that carpeted the bottom of the lake, glimmers light up and rise towards the surface, dragging long, milky filaments after them. They were medusae moving in spirals, illuminating the frazil like stained glass before pulverizing it in their vortices.

A gust of wind carried the distant notes of music coming from the opposite wing – an endlessly repeating monotonous tune. I also heard animated voices, all talking at the same time. I thought that the benefactors were giving a party for the protégées but then changed my mind because it became apparent that the pleasure was one-sided. The protégées didn't appear to find anything amusing. Beneath their piercing cries, protestations, tears, and supplications roared the unwavering laughter of the benefactors. This laughter, the same as that which had enjoyed my punishment, was more nauseating than the lake's foul stench conveyed by the wind.

I quickly closed the garret window and went to bed. My bed was not comfortable. The sheets were like ice. I felt miserable, and if I'd had lacrimal glands, I surely would've cried. I found some consolation in the thought that perhaps my fate was better than that of the protégées.

I was put to work at the crack of dawn the next day with a floor brush and bucket, as well as a list of tasks that could be done on hands and knees: washing the kitchen and bathroom tiles, scrubbing the hardwood floor of the refectory, brushing the carpets of the dormitory, polishing shoes, sweeping the ashes from the fireplaces, scouring the andirons, dusting the baseboards, cleaning the stairs ... nothing too drastically unfamiliar to someone used to inferiority.

I was about to start buffing the flagstones of the entrance hall when the headmistress, owl on her fist, came to tell me that the benefactors had taken my father's body back to the city.

"Your family is devastated, of course. The funeral will be held tomorrow in the presence of all the university faculty, and you are urged not to attend."

She then outlined, in the same breath, the list of rules I'd have to follow from now on. With her index, she pointed to the doors around the hall, shaking the set of keys that hung on her belt, which sounded like bones rattling.

"You are strictly forbidden from entering the boardroom and the benefactors' wing, and you'll be severely punished if you go near them. As for the front door, it would be useless to try to open it: it's always double-locked for the safety of our protégées."

I asked her if there were bears in the area. The question annoyed her, and she made a dry click with her black tongue.

"The lake is dangerous. Its shores are eroded by quicksand. The water descends to unfathomable depths where light can't penetrate. It's murky but far from dormant: its whirlpools can sink a boat in a heartbeat, and it swarms with venomous medusae. Our protégées know better than to look in that direction. You'd be wise to do the same."

She started circling me, grabbing my arm every time she lost her footing, practically taking me down with her. From time to time, the owl spat out one of those repugnant pellets of undigested bone and fur that raptors regurgitate.

"You didn't cry or bat an eyelid yesterday," the headmistress hissed in my ear. "You have a very rare gift, Medusa. A remarkable gift! It would be a shame if something bad were to happen to you ..."

There was so much malice in her voice that I suspected, on the contrary, that she wanted me to get sucked into the abyss with the algae and medusae. But instead of frightening me, she only piqued my curiosity. The lake held many mysteries, and I vowed to be on the lookout.

The institute's thirteen protégées were slightly older than me. They all shared the same dormitory, took their meals in silence at the large table in the refectory, and spent their days together in the study hall.

As you might expect, the Athenaeum had nothing in common with the illustrious academy except its name. No teacher taught here. The protégées had no desks, pencils, notebooks, or textbooks. They learned no history, grammar, philosophy, mathematics, not even music or home economics.

A few books lined the shelves of the study hall, but the selection was limited to fairy tales and romance novels. Otherwise, the room was littered with broken, old toys, chipped and mismatched toy tea sets, one-eyed dolls in dollhouses with wobbly furniture, puzzles with missing pieces, and used colouring books. Don't ask me how the protégées killed time in this children's playroom.

A quartet of matrons supervised them from morning till night. Keeping strict order like wardens, they broke up conversations before they could become confabs. They ensured the rows were straight, inspected uniforms and fingernails, took note of any misbehaviour in a black binder, administered the punishment decreed by the headmistress ... They were also responsible for the front doors, checking that they were locked at all times and, accompanied by the watchdogs, stood guard at night. The fob watches they wore pinned to their chests were synchronized to the second.

Every afternoon, rain or shine, the protégées would take the air in the back courtyard – a square of gravel with no view of the lake. The refectory window also looked out onto this courtyard, and one day, while I was cleaning up the remains from lunch, I took the opportunity to observe them during their recess.

Spring had finally come and the sun beamed down, making some of them unbutton their schoolgirl coats. Their hairstyles were identical: two braids tied with red ribbons. Jabbering away, they skipped rope, played hopscotch or hoops, stopping only to squabble. They had high-pitched voices and a childish way of putting their hands over their mouths when they laughed.

One of the protégées, too small to play with her companions, stood apart. She was what is called a little person – someone who develops in miniature. She had a regular face, straight back, proportional limbs, but she was so tiny that some might take her for a doll. She had a cheerful, pretty countenance, and her kitten eyes sparkled with mischievous excitement. Her glossy hair wasn't braided, in contrast to the other protégées: it had been hacked off and crowned her like a tousled halo. She was busy knitting a minuscule bonnet and didn't seem to give a damn about being excluded from the group.

You couldn't confuse the protégées with children, however: their bodies were already in their prime, some of them even had generous curves. As for the deficiencies in conformity that had necessitated their incarceration in this institute, it was hard not to notice them: they stuck out in plain view. A skull shaped like a sugarloaf. A strawberry birthmark covering the entire face. Rheumy crossed eyes. A cleft lip split to the nostrils. A Pulcinella hump on the back. Elephantine ears. An extended chin. A protruding tongue thicker than a calf's. An equinus foot. A hand with webbed fingers. A missing nose. A head slumped over a rubbery neck …

Despite the pity I felt for these sufferers of nature, I couldn't stand looking at them any longer and quickly moved away from the window. The end-of-recess bell rang and before a matron could surprise me, I turned back to my work, still haunted by memories of the protégées.

For an eye that naturally looks for symmetry and harmony of form, the malformations of these girls would be frightening. Yet the headmistress had judged that my Disgustingnesses were even worse. In that case, they must be of such repugnitude that they could shatter mirrors.

Once a month, on the night of the new moon, the boarders received a visit from the benefactors. For the occasion, they dressed up in organza puff dresses and white socks and coiled their braids over their ears, which gave them an even more juvenile appearance. They spent those nights in the private wing and only came out at dawn the next day, their dresses filthy and torn, their hair loose, their cheeks covered in tears – and their lips completely blackened like those of the headmistress.

I'd hear the matrons complain about the mess that reigned over the place after these nocturnal parties. Their references to the rampages and escapades of the benefactors left me perplexed; the double entendres and innuendoes of their remarks sounded like gobbledygook. Overcome by curiosity, I'd lose myself in speculations but was still so innocent that I couldn't imagine anything worse than what I'd suffered in the boardroom.

Despite the headmistress's interdiction, I approached the forbidden door and tried to peek through the keyhole countless times – yet without managing to make out much of anything. The chance to catch a glimpse of what hid behind it came one evening, just before the benefactors' arrival …

The headmistress's owl had once again regurgitated pellets, and I was sent urgently to the entrance hall to clean the floor. I grabbed the bucket and floorcloth and rushed to pick up the vile pellets. Then I noticed a triangle of light on the black basalt filtering in from the benefactors' wing: the forbidden door had been left ajar. Pressed by the fear of being caught red-handed, I quickly slipped my head through the door and parted my bangs to see better.

The bare aspect of the protégées' wing was a stark contrast to the clutter of the benefactors' one, judging by the long corridor that stretched before me, decked from floor to ceiling with paintings and display cases assembling an impressive collection of collections, clearly labelled with engraved brass plates. Torn stamps, crumbling insects, mismatched sports cards, bits of string, broken lead soldiers, chewing-gum wrappers, pocket knives with chipped blades, pieces of airplane models, all amassed by the benefactors in their child-hood and generously donated to the institute.

There was something sinister about these piles of broken souvenirs, in how they were arranged in untidy sets and displayed as nostalgic trophies. Besides the maniacal character of their collectors, this immoderate accumulation implied an inability to let go of the past and a need to box up what was damaged. It couldn't help but recall the collection of deformities stored in the protégées' wing ...

I was so absorbed in my observations that I didn't hear a matron barge into the hall and head towards me. I felt her meathook grab my shoulder and turned around with a start. While my distraught hands were awkwardly trying to rearrange my bangs over my Repulsivities, the matron had a violent reaction: her face turned green, her knees started to shake, and from her bewildered mouth, a pulpy mass of chyme and bile spewed out and splattered on the flagstones.

I didn't wait for the command before starting to clean up the mess I'd caused.

As soon as she was told of my infraction, the head-mistress imposed her first penalty: she locked me up in a cubbyhole for the whole night. Located under the cellar stairs, the cubbyhole was so cramped I had to roll into a ball to fit in. Once the door was shut, not one particle of light filtered into the darkness, but all I had to do was dilate my pupils to see the brambles, nettles, thistles, and poison ivy making up the bedding that had been laid out for me. My night vision sharpened even more: I had no trouble distinguishing the nettle hair, sharp thorns, and poisonous exudates.

The headmistress had confiscated my dress and left me with only a thin slip for protection. In no time, my skin was riddled with scratches, blisters, and ooz-ing sores. The tiniest movement exacerbated the sharp pain caused by my ulcerations. The memory of my humiliation before the matron stung even more: I was so ashamed to have been caught naked-eyed that I would've been content to remain shut in the cubbyhole for the rest of my days and never face anyone again.

I first tried to console myself by spacing out but couldn't do it. Then I closed my lids and rubbed them hard enough to hurt my ocular globes – and realized that my pain diminished. The burning and itching sensation subsided and was replaced by a caressing, comforting warmth, gentle and restful.

By this providential fortuity, I discovered another ability of my Abhorrencies: their analgesic effect. By taking refuge behind my lids, I could lessen physical pain and almost completely anaesthetize myself. So I slept curled up on the quilt of thorns and needles with the abandon of a fakir on a bed of nails.

My sleep was so profound that the headmistress had to shake me awake when she came to free me at dawn the next morning. She inspected the wounds on my arms, legs, and hands and was surprised to find me fresh, alert, and impassive when I should've suffered like a martyr.

"You're not even scratching yourself," she said, pursing her black lips. "It's really remarkable!"

While the protégées were still with the benefactors, she sent me to the dormitory to change the sheets.

"Make sure you finish before they return. Then wash the matron's dress until every last vomit stain is gone. But before letting you go, we have to take some precautions."

She had brought a horse bridle with her, which she stuck on my head, tugging on the leather straps. The blinders on each side hid my eyes behind their opaque screens.

"This way, everyone will be safer," the headmistress said.

My peripheral vision, already fairly limited, was even more restricted by the imposition of these blinders that were as uncomfortable as they were cumbersome, and whose incongruity made the grotesque nature of my Encumbrances even more obvious. In their stiff leather vice, my field of vision was so narrow that I had to compensate by frequent neck twists and much back cracking.

Thus harnessed, I quickly made my way to the dormitory. Just like the refectory, it was a rectangular room whose windows looked onto the back courtyard. Thirteen beds with white bedspreads were staggered on either side of the central aisle; each one was matched with a dresser on which stood a toiletry bag.

Blinded by my ocular screens, I didn't notice that one of the beds was occupied. I was so surprised to hear a voice speak near me that I dropped the pile of sheets I'd brought from the laundry. The voice was thin and clear: "You're the one they call Medusa?"

I saw two swinging legs not touching the floor and so recognized the miniature girl with chopped hair. She was sitting on the edge of the mattress with her hands between her knees. I was so shocked that she'd spoken to me that my voice came out of my throat like a bark.

"What are you doing here? Why aren't you at the party with the others?"

She pulled out her hands and started twisting her nightgown.

"We're not allowed to present ourselves before the benefactors when we're indisposed. I stained the sheet. I'm sorry."

Her name was Suzanne. In contrast to the other protégées, she had no other deficiency in conformity besides her size.

"The girls ostracize me because I'm not like them. I cut my hair to make myself uglier, in solidarity. The headmistress was furious with me, the benefactors even more so: they like hair they can pull ..."

While I changed the sheets, she told me that she'd been found by nuns when she was a baby and had grown up in an orphanage. She had been unhappy there and treated with severity because she kept trying to run away. She couldn't believe her luck when, one fine Sunday, she was summoned to the parlour and presented to a wealthy shipowner who wanted to adopt her, despite the fact that she was already fifteen. She'd been charmed by the distinguished gentleman and had followed him to his car in a scamper.

"I thought I'd found a family at last, but my new father, who is one of the benefactors of this institute, soon abandoned me here. I see him only once every twenty-eight days, when he comes to attend the board meetings and participate in the nocturnal games, which are always held on the new moon. You see, the benefactors want us to have the carefree attitude of children and think that at this time, there is less chance of us menstruating."

I thought of the nighttime cries of the protégées.

"What games do they play, exactly?"

"Games that are not appropriate for their age. My adoptive father, for example, likes to jump on beds and have pillow fights. Then, he'll lie down with his cuddly toys. There's a pile in the resting room: teddy bears, plush horses, lions, cats, Pekinese ... To help him fall asleep, I have to dress up like a lamb and jump over him so he can count sheep. And as soon as he begins to snore, I have to watch him sleep without blinking. Sometimes I hate this place so much I actually miss the orphanage."

She looked so downcast that I tried to cheer her up.

"Maybe your adoptive father will end up taking you around the world on one of his cargo ships ..."

"Unlikely," she said. "He's already told me that a merchant ship is too dangerous a place for a young girl – especially one as small as me. And anyway, what would my life with him be? The life of a nightlight! No, thanks."

Suzanne wanted to give me a hand with the sheets, but I refused: she might have accidentally caught a glimpse of my Miseries, and I had no intention of making such a nice person throw up. Before I left, she told me, "We might be at the bottom of the ladder of this institute, Medusa, but that doesn't mean we have to keep being their scapegoats. One day, we'll escape."

I was surprised and really moved that she wanted to take me with her. As I was leaving the dormitory, I realized that she'd made no comment about my blinders, and the sympathy I felt for her was doubled by gratitude. I had found an ally.

I spent the next five years on all fours, hands plunged in soapy water, hair covered in dust. The matrons never said a word to me; I didn't eat with them but by the stove, out of a porringer.

The blinders made a frame from which I couldn't get out, so I got used to perceiving the world in fragments, without ever grasping the whole. For me, this didn't represent a significant narrowing of perspective.

I tried to disappear into the woodwork by redoubling my efforts to accomplish my tasks, the list of which got increasingly long. I crouched by the baseboards, burrowed under the furniture. Out of sheer repetition, I perfected the movements I made: the ebb and flow of the rags, the oscillation of the brush, the swaying of the scrubbing pad, the to-and-fro of the mop, the swinging of the feather duster ... My hands were chapped and my nails broken. My knees, with their buildup of blisters, became callous.

I learned to work like a mouse, without making the smallest sound, because the headmistress, increasingly neurasthenic, couldn't tolerate the friction of a broom against the floor, or the rustle of a rag on the furniture, or the sloshing of water in a bucket. The full moon gave her migraines, which carved dark circles under her eyes and which she tried to alleviate by putting a damp cloth on top of her bald head. On those days, she consumed only white food: rice pudding, tapioca, cream of wheat, and other boiled mush. She would take refuge in the boardroom, where, I later learned, she'd sink nostalgically into the Athenaeum's archives.

She always came out of her hole with lips as black as liquorice and in an even darker mood. I would quickly fall under her strict rule and have to obey her insatiable demands. She'd track down my derelictions of duty with the utmost scrupulousness and invariably find them. Victorious at catching me in the wrong, she'd let out a eureka of satisfaction and send me to sleep in the cubbyhole. It was all the same to me. At least there, I had the nettles to comfort me – and a chance to use my night vision.

Once, I managed to receive the headmistress's approval. As recompense, she gave me a new responsibility.

"It's a task perfectly suited for someone used to grovelling," she indicated.

This is how I started taking care of her owl. I cleaned the droppings from the aviary – an octagonal cage with a zinc roof, located to the right of the main entrance, outside the benefactors' wing. To feed the raptor, I set up traps around the boarding school and caught field mice, muskrats, chipmunks, shrews, sometimes even martens ... I'd cut the creatures in two and put them in the feeder every evening at dusk.

Like all barred owls, the headmistress's bird was far-sighted and wouldn't recognize the carrion I put in front of it without having first felt it with its claws and vibrissae. It would then tear it apart, raising its head from time to time with a bloody morsel hanging from its beak.

The particular placement of its eyes, not on the sides but in the centre of the face, greatly limited its visual field – especially since its enormous ocular globes were fixed. Its neck, however, was incredibly flexible and could pivot to such a degree that it could see behind it without moving its body. Given my blinders, I could've really used a neck like that.

The owl's pupils were so dilated that its eyes looked like two obsidian marbles. I wondered if mine looked like that too, if their dilation explained the acuity of my night vision. Owls, however, don't see anything in pitch darkness. While I could even distinguish colours now.

On the nights of the parties, I'd go to the lit-up windows and try to spy on what was happening in the benefactors' wing. My curiosity was never appeased, though, because the curtains were always drawn. Although my Revoltingnesses could pierce the darkness, they couldn't go through fabric – at least, not yet.

I didn't get a chance to see Suzanne very often during these miserable years. Sometimes, I'd cross her in the corridor, where she'd be sent to stand in a corner for frequent misbehaviour, but she was always kept under watch by a matron, and it was impossible to communicate with her other than through knowing glances.

I found her alone at last, one May morning, perched on a chair in the study hall. This time, the headmistress had given her detention for a serious offence: the little busybody had broken into the boardroom and been caught nosing around the library, which held a collection of works on a range of subjects amassed and bequeathed to the Athenaeum by none other than the venerable founder.

"The headmistress warned me that she won't be so lenient next time," Suzanne told me with an unrepentant shrug. "She was so upset by my sacrilege she didn't even notice that I'd filched a couple of books right under her nose!"

The books in question must've been part of one of those ancient travelling libraries, since they fit in the palm of one hand; their kid-leather binding was so dried up it was crumbling to dust. One book described the world's greatest escapes in history. Suzanne had started reading the first chapter, which recounted the spectacular getaway of an old libertine via the lead roofs of the palace where he was being held prisoner. The story had made a big impression on her.

"If it's possible to escape a dungeon, then why not an institute?" she asked me, grabbing my hands. "Let's run away tonight, Medusa! After all, what keeps us here?"

"And where will we go?"

"To another city where the benefactors will never be able to track us down. We'll find some kind of work to live. Worst case, we'll become beggars ..."

She started hatching plans of escape with such unruly enthusiasm it made me dizzy. She didn't seem to realize that I wasn't free, like her, to mix with normal people. With my Disfigurations, I'd be greeted with insults and cries of terror everywhere. Scorned by all, how would I manage to have a roof over my head and earn my daily bread? I had to face facts: the institute was my only refuge in this world.

But I was too ashamed to admit all this to Suzanne. Instead, I tried to discourage her. I told her that it was madness. That we'd never be able to open the doors. That even if we got out through the windows, the dogs would jump us as soon as our feet touched the ground. That we'd be too easily spotted on the road. That we'd get lost in the forest. That even if we managed to escape, the benefactors, being powerful men, would set sleuth hounds on our trail ...

My insistent objections got the better of her fanciful ideas. Discouragement overcame her. She pushed away the book on escapes with disdain and slipped the other into my hand.

"Here, take it. I stole it for you."

Through my hair, I clearly saw that she had tears in her eyes. I felt so bad about causing her pain that I made her a reckless promise.

"Don't give up hope. I'll find a way to get us out of here …"

The opuscule that Suzanne had given me bore, in half-faded gold lettering, the unequivocal title *The Naughty History of Olympus*. No one had ever opened it and, lacking a letter opener, I had to use a nail file to separate the folded pages of laid paper.

I read it that very evening, absorbing it in broad strokes, like a dog lapping a bowl of water. My Nightmarishnesses swung back and forth with an uninterrupted motion, following the axis of the lines, taking in the words. Even without light, my dilated pupils had no trouble making out the printed text, although the type was very small.

The book's author, who had chosen to remain anonymous, recounted in vivid detail and with a lascivious pen various salacious stories from Greek mythology: Europa's frolics with the white bull; Danaë's intoxication in the golden rain; Leda's frantic lovemaking against the swan's long neck; Eurymedousa's indiscretions with the ant; Io's ecstasy in the thick blanket of clouds ... The descriptions of his heroines' anatomy were certainly instructive, but nonetheless somewhat disappointing – at least for me – because the author never focussed on their eyes.

My waning interest perked up when I saw the word *Medusa* as the chapter heading. I slowed down my reading pace to better appreciate the episode of her metamorphosis – you might not know this, but Medusa didn't start out a monster. The daughter of sea gods, she was the youngest of the Gorgons and the most beautiful of the three sisters; in fact, her hair was her favourite attribute and she'd spend hours in front of the mirror combing it and rubbing it with essential oils. To her great misfortune, she aroused Poseidon's passion. The impetuous sea god ambushed her while she was alone in the temple of Athena. Like a tidal wave, he fell upon her, pinned her against a column, and, deaf to her pleas for mercy, raped her. (A dramatic scene that the author depicted bluntly and not without a certain relish in the racy tone of which he was so fond.)

Alerted by the cries of her owl, Athena discovered the coital profanation of her sanctuary and became infuriated by this crime of lèse-divinité. For some reason whose logic escapes me, the goddess pardoned the guilty party and punished the three Gorgons. She gave them a horrible appearance with heads of writhing serpents, boar tusks, lolling tongues, skin covered in scales, bronze hands, and convergent eyes. She also endowed Medusa with the power to turn to stone any man who dared to gaze upon her.

Closing the book, I wondered whether my Dreadfulnesses had a similar petrifying power and whether I'd actually transformed my father's heart into stone ... This patricidal thought disturbed me, and to chase it away, I shut my burning lids and clenched them tight, so much that my eardrums throbbed from the pressure. I rubbed their thick-lipped folds by rolling the dense, bushy lashes under my fingers. Instead of mollifying me, the friction produced an itch similar to the kind you feel before sneezing – a terrible, tingling sensation that I didn't try to soothe but instead exacerbated with ardent curiosity.

The sensation was more intense in the inner angle of the palpebral slit. Since my lacrimal caruncles were dry, I moistened them with a bit of saliva and pressed them under my thumbs. The fleshy nodules hardened when I crushed them between my nails. They were simultaneously the source and focal point of a climax whose density engulfed me. My body was in the throes of such excitement that the rush of pleasure shot through my spine to the curve of my sacrum like a bolt of lightning. Electrified by a fierce current, my optical nerves started to crackle and I saw sparks.

When I opened my Onanisms, my fingers were sticky with blood – the blood of my first monstruation.

One evening, I was in the aviary spreading fresh litter on the floor when the owl started hooting and fidgeting on its perch. It was July: the lake stagnated in the suffocating heat; the sky was grey from the humidity; the threat of an imminent storm darkened the landscape. Encumbered by my bridle, it took some time before I could identify what had alarmed the owl: the incongruous sight of a rowboat moving away from the shore.

I immediately recognized the stocky silhouettes of the two matrons rowing. Sitting silently side by side, tilting their bodies forward to make themselves small, they were pulling so hard at the oars while also trying to avoid making any splashing noises that I thought they might be trying to escape – especially since they were transporting a large, formless bundle wrapped in burlap, which resembled baggage.

I stepped out of the aviary so intrigued that I forgot to close the gate. Crouching behind a tree, I pulled back my blinders to better observe the matrons, who were nearing a whirlpool. How could they be risking their lives like this after the headmistress's repeated warnings against the dangerous water?

They soon brought the boat to a standstill, however. Struggling to keep their balance, they raised the heavy bundle and threw it overboard. They swayed back and forth for a moment and grabbed hold of the stern so as not to tip over, then quickly took up the oars to row back to shore. After mooring the rowboat behind a clump of reeds, they walked back to the institute on the double.

As for the bundle of burlap, it had sunk straight down, leaving a torpid eddy in its wake in which the medusae swirled, dragging their twisting, entangled filaments behind their opalescent globes. Caught in this luminescent vortex, hairlike algae glittered in the black water. It looked as though a giant eye had just opened in the middle of the night.

The matrons must've had a truly heinous secret to have taken such extreme measures to rid themselves of it. I wanted to get closer to better see the bottom of the lake, but I'd barely gone ten steps before I was intercepted by the pack of dogs.

I'd been betrayed by the owl, who had escaped the aviary and alerted the household. Fur bristled, jowls curled back, the dogs the headmistress had set on me were ready to attack. My reaction to their threat was purely instinctual: I showed them my Unspeakables.

The watchdogs immediately submitted, bellies to the ground, ears flattened, whimpering plaintively. I felt pity for the poor beasts and retreated to the institute's doors. The headmistress was waiting for me on the threshold, her owl informant on her fist. Pale with vexation, she handed me a wood box that she held with her fingertips.

"I forbade you to go near the lake. You disobeyed me, and for this you get your second warning."

The box held a necklace of large felt balls that had

the colour of raw linen and the vicious appearance of mohair. All over, shrivelled, yellow-bristled vermicular forms of an indeterminate nature were stuck in the fibres. The headmistress explained:

"These are cocoons of the processionary caterpillar, whose urticating hairs itch like mad and leave the skin covered in raw blisters and sores that take months to heal. You'll wear this necklace until further notice. And since you're so skilled at handling the dogs, you'll take care of them from now on, too."

By the time I got back to my room that night, my skin was already burning from the cocoons, the fire stoked by the necklace rubbing on my nape, shoulders, and chest. Despite the pain, I didn't close my eyes. I sat up in the garret window, trying to spot the bundle at the bottom of the lake.

The storm had broken out and flashes of lightning intermittently lit up the rain-riddled surface. The whirlpool had closed in on itself, the medusae had extinguished their lights. The lake was so murky that even when I opened my Chasms wide, I could barely penetrate the turbid water.

I was interrupted by someone scratching at my door and barely had time to rearrange my hair over my face before Suzanne's nose peeked through the crack. Having been kept up by a stubborn insomnia, she'd heard the matrons talking about my latest infraction and terrible punishment. As soon as the coast was clear, she'd slipped out of the dormitory to check up on me. With a light step, she joined me at the garret window.

"Do you know that this is the first time I've seen the lake since I came to the institute? The dormitory and study-hall windows all face the forest, and the trees are my only horizon when we go out at recess."

The pleasure of seeing her was eclipsed by the fear of what would happen to her if she got caught.

"You shouldn't be here. Go back to bed!"

"Don't worry. With all this thunder, the matrons aren't likely to hear me. Here, I brought something to console you."

She slipped a black tablet into my hand that might have passed for liquorice if it weren't for its pungent odour – a peppery smell of damp flint.

"It's resin," Suzanne said. "Make sure to chew it well if you want to get the full effect. It won't ease the pain, unfortunately, but you'll no longer care about anything."

I put the tablet on my tongue, a bit repulsed by its acridity. The resin had the consistency of balsam-fir gum; chewing it, I felt sandy grains crunch between my teeth. However, the taste was not unpleasant: a mix of hay, soil, and turpentine. I savoured it while listening to Suzanne chatter.

"My adoptive father smuggles resin from the distant places he travels to and supplies the headmistress free of charge. She's gotten addicted to it and takes it in secret. She thinks we know nothing about it, but her black teeth give her away."

On the nights of the parties, the headmistress would distribute a handful of tablets to all the protégées, so that they'd go along with the benefactors' games without making a fuss. To the oversensitive ones, she'd have to give a double dose; if they continued to cry and complain, they'd be summoned to the headmistress's office one fine morning, sent away from the institute, and never be heard from again.

"In fact, the humpback vanished yesterday and she'll

soon be replaced by someone new. It's true that she was constantly bawling her eyes out. She left without anyone noticing – without saying goodbye, without even taking her personal effects. I wonder what will happen to her. Maybe she'll be cloistered in a convent, or shut into an asylum, or sold off to a madam in lower town. If she's lucky, she'll be thrown out on the streets and reduced to begging on corners ..."

Suzanne had assured me that the resin would dull my senses. Yet it seemed that my perceptions were made even sharper by the tranquillizing effect: in fact, I was acutely aware not only of the slightest sensation on my skin (which made the urticating necklace even more uncomfortable) but also of every facet of reality. I scrutinized the landscape with sustained attention, noticing the slightest variations in the ambient humidity, measuring every roll of thunder and note of rain. Thus deconstructed, the world seemed more comprehensible to me.

At last, my gaze settled on the lake, penetrated its shimmering surface, slowly slid down to the muddy bottom. Through the algae, duckweed, and suspended sediment, I finally distinguished a burlap bundle. Then two. Then three ... There were about fifteen in total, in various states of decomposition, scattered along the rippled bottom like tomb effigies in a sunken cemetery.

Lying thus, the sacks took on undoubtedly human form. And among them, I recognized the Pulcinella hump of the protégée who had disappeared the previous night. I also distinguished tied feet, bound bodies, bloated heads, hair escaping through ripped burlap, remains of facial features with devoured eye sockets, dismantled jaws, flesh bloated and blistered from prolonged exposure to water. The lake was full of cadavers!

Imagine my utter dismay. I had discovered the Athenaeum's most terrible secret: no boarder ever came out alive. As soon as the girls ceased amusing the benefactors, they'd be sacrificed, their bodies weighed down and thrown into the water. They'd end up forgotten in an abyssal grave, left to the indignity of being macerated and picked apart by medusae. They'd never rest in peace, because the whirlpool would drag them forever into its coven of the damned. And this was why the vapours emanating from this charnel house were so fetid.

My thoughts, usually faltering, coursed at full speed in my mind, branching off into various agonizing conjectures while Suzanne kept chatting beside me, "I intend to do everything I can to displease the benefactors in the hopes that I too will be sent away."

My blood froze when I heard this – and I was forced to share my suspicions with her. After calculating the probability of suffering a fate similar to that of the entombed protégées if we stayed at the institute, we quickly came to the conclusion that we had to run away as soon as possible. We then assessed various escape plans and our chances of success, which were all pretty slim. Out of sheer desperation, I suggested, "There's a village at the other end of the lake. I can see the bell tower on clear days. We could reach it by rowboat and find shelter there ... Then, we'll surely find some charitable soul who can help us get to the train station."

Suzanne approved the plan immediately and started preparing: "The ideal moment will be during the next nocturnal party. I don't know the first thing about handling boats, but there's an introductory manual in the library. I'll bring it with me. You'll be in charge of provisions. By the time the matrons notice our absence, we'll already be far away, and they won't have any means of following us."

I assured her that the dogs wouldn't be a problem and that I'd come looking for her at the next new moon.

The following days were truly torturous. I was on hot coals of anticipation, in addition to enduring the cauterizing sting of the cocoons every time my Scandal-ousities had to stay open – when feeding the hounds, for example.

I now commanded the watchdogs' respect: they wouldn't dare come near me, even when I was giving them food. I'd take advantage of this to look at the lake and make sure that the rowboat was still moored in the reeds. And I'd inspect the interminable waning of the gibbous moon.

It all would've been easier to tolerate if it weren't for the headmistress's incessant surveillance, never letting me out of her sight and constantly pestering me with her persnickety nitpicking. It was as if she suspected that something was up and was determined to force me to reveal my intentions. But I had nothing to fear: she was simply tracking my resistance to pain. She kept saying, "It's remarkable, simply remarkable!"

The owl echoed her with its hooting.

After one week, she let me take off the necklace and put it back in its box.

"The next time you misbehave, I'll have to send you away. And I'd be surprised if your family took you back ..." she gently reminded me.

I knew very well where she was threatening to send me. I was even more determined, therefore, not to remain at the institute long enough to deserve a third warning.

On the nights of the parties, as soon as the protégées were locked in the benefactors' private wing, the matrons would retire to their rooms, taking advantage of their time off to go to bed early. As for the headmistress, she'd already be well into an advanced and altered state of resinous stupor. Only the dogs and owl stood guard over the institute. This was the moment we'd chosen for our escape.

In order to be exempted from the party, Suzanne had pretended to have her period. She was waiting for me in the dormitory, bag under her arm.

I opened the window without making too much noise, lifted one leg over the sill, and landed in the grass on two feet. The air was fresh and damp, the darkness thick. The watchdogs immediately came running, but I removed my blinders and they were quickly grovelling at my feet, servile and penitent.

I helped Suzanne descend by making her a short ladder, since the window was too high for her. Then led her by the hand to the lakeshore.

"We're free!" she said, jumping with joy.

Though there was no moon, the lake was illuminated by the medusae. I settled Suzanne in the rowboat and cast off, forgetting that my face was uncovered and that she could see my Unapproachables. I realized it when she turned her eyes away, her face crimson with embarrassment.

I tried to hide behind my hair, but it was too late. Suzanne was already pulling at the oars, valiantly though a bit erratically due to the limited length of her arms and legs, which barely touched the bottom. Scared out of her wits, she rushed to increase the distance between us. She was already out of reach, and I didn't know how to swim.

I stayed on the shore, watching the rowboat disappear into the distance, mortified by being abandoned, cursing my Menaces, which had just cost me both friendship and freedom.

The dogs suddenly lifted their heads and started growling. In the middle of the lake, the water began making a circular movement. The vortex grew larger, twisted into a funnel, ready to engulf Suzanne who, lost in the darkness, was heading straight for it. I shouted at her to warn her of the danger, which only made her row even harder.

Around the boat, the medusae were pulsating their glaucous glow. They formed a perfect circle and splashed their umbrella-shaped bells as though at a funeral dance. Their sinuous filaments twisted around the oars, immobilizing them. When Suzanne tried to shake them free, they came out of the oarlocks and slipped out of her hands.

The watchdogs were barking, the owl was hooting. I didn't hear the doors of the institute open, or the matrons running over with their flashlights, or the headmistress come out just in time to see the rowboat capsize and Suzanne go overboard.

She didn't know how to swim, either. She didn't even have time to cry out before going under. The water closed over her, and the whirlpool vanished like a mirage does when you get close to it. The lake's surface regained its steady calm, leaving behind no trace of the tragedy except the overturned, drifting rowboat.

The medusae illuminated the lake bottom, where the vortex had sucked in poor Suzanne. I didn't get a chance to see her miniature body join the cadavers of the other protégées, because two matrons grabbed me each by one arm and dragged me back to the institute. In any case, I wouldn't have had the courage to look.

Meanwhile, in the benefactors' wing, the party was still in full swing, as though nothing had happened. On the steps, the headmistress was chewing her resin with the vehemence of a raptor's beak. She dismissed the matrons and grabbed me by the arm.

"Wait till you see what punishment I have in store for you."

My Aridities had not shed a tear at my father's death. Why would they have cried any more at Suzanne's? The impossibility of lacrimally manifesting my sorrow exacerbated my feeling of guilt. I was devastated by having caused the loss of the only person who had ever shown me any fellow feeling – even, dare I say, the only friend I'd ever had. If I hadn't inspired such horror in her, Suzanne wouldn't have fled and wouldn't have sunk, by the cruellest twist of irony, into the very tomb I was trying to help her avoid ...

I had plenty of time to self-flagellate with these rebukes, since the headmistress made me languish in the entrance hall. On all fours, I crawled around aimlessly on the basalt flagstones, indifferent to the punishment that awaited me, certain that I deserved the worst treatment.

In this regard, the headmistress didn't disappoint me. She returned with a bucket, setting it down before me so I could see what was inside: a grey, gelatinous mass entangled with threads too numerous to count.

"You resisted the brambles, nettles, thistles, and processionary cocoons. Let's see how you tolerate what I fished out of our lake for you ..."

She slipped on her falconry glove and plunged her hand into the bucket. She extracted a medusa, lifting it by its bell.

"See these filaments? They're covered with minuscule vesicles in the shape of harpoons that shatter like glass upon contact with the skin. The venom they inject spreads through the nerves."

She made me roll up my dress sleeves and expose my forearms to the filaments. They barely grazed the skin, and I thought I would faint. I can't describe the pain other than suggesting the corrosion of lemon juice on flesh lacerated by barbed wire. The headmistress said in a flat voice, "As you can see, the venom is still formidably virulent even when the medusa is dead."

Without further ado, she proved it. The first blow stung, especially since the second wasn't far behind. I shut my lids at once and squeezed them tight over my ocular globes. At the third blow, I felt nothing more than the caressing warmth of sunlight filtering through branches.

Seeing my impassiveness, the headmistress made me take off my dress and worked herself to death thrashing my back with the medusa. When she started flogging my posterior, I was barely able to stifle a groan of well-being.

A kind of euphoria had taken hold of me, because I now had proof that my Viciousnesses could not only transform pain into pleasure, but also that the intensification of one increased the other tenfold.

The headmistress stopped, gasping for breath, and ordered me to stand up. For years, I'd crawled before her, completely bent over, and could hardly believe that I was now her height. My body was much more developed than hers, however, and my figure bore down on hers.

After taking off her sticky glove, she made me turn around a few times, inspecting me from head to foot.

"I've been observing you for years, and I've never heard you complain. I impose the most severe punishment on you and expect you to cry, but the tears never come. And now you laugh when you should be howling. Tell me, what's your secret?"

I wasn't about to confide in her, so I just shrugged.

"I close my eyes, that's all."

She let out a small hooting sound that sent chills down my spine.

"You have a very rare talent, Medusa. A talent I wish I'd had in my younger years. You're far too precious to be sent back to your mother, who probably wouldn't take you anyway. What do you think about putting down your apron and becoming one of the institute's protégées?"

Without waiting for my answer, she went on, "The other girls are chickens and crybabies, to one degree or another. The benefactors therefore have to curb their enthusiasm, which isn't that amusing for them. But you, Medusa, with your tolerance for pain, you'll be the ideal playmate."

She helped me to get dressed, whispering tender words in my ear. She promised that I'd be excused from work and could read all day long, and once a month, I'd spend the night with the benefactors with no task other than amusing them.

"There is no greater calling than dedicating yourself to the benefactors," she said with feverish exaltation. "Tomorrow, you'll move into my rooms. I'll take charge of your apprenticeship and, at the next new moon, present you to the board."

I went up to my garret at a loss, not knowing whether I should rejoice or worry about this radical change in attitude towards me. The curiosity that the benefactors' wing had initially inspired in me had turned to fear, and the dangers that lurked there didn't give me any reassurance. Nevertheless, I went up to the garret window and, before Suzanne's grave, swore I'd leave this place alive.

Despite the riotous life the headmistress had dangled before me, it quickly became apparent that it was much more wearisome to be her darling than her underling. She now devoted herself entirely to my person and wouldn't give me more than a moment's rest.

Miraculously cured of her migraines, she'd regained her appetite and now rarely fell into a state of languor, since she almost never chewed resin. No tinge of remorse, no thoughts of Suzanne or the other disappeared boarders seemed to distract her from her main preoccupation: transforming me into a protégée who could please the benefactors, her respect for whom was almost as fanatical as her adoration of the founder.

Ever since she'd taken me under her wing, I slept in the bedroom next to hers, and when I woke up in the morning, I'd find her at the foot of my bed with the owl on her fist. She'd serve me breakfast, wash and groom me, and struggle to brush my hair somehow.

My old rags had been thrown away; I now wore the same schoolgirl tunic as the protégées. As for the blinders, they'd been replaced by a blindfold tied at the back of my head, which the headmistress had made from one of her black knitted stockings and which was so opaque that it was impossible to see through.

"Best to be cautious," she'd say every morning as she

pulled and adjusted the knots of the blindfold. "Accidents happen faster than you think."

I'd been relieved of my household chores but had no time to read, because now I had to get used to living without the aid of my Ghastlinesses. It was blindly, therefore, that I explored the benefactors' wing, trying to find my way around the rooms that gave off the corridor I'd already glimpsed, with its display cases full of collections.

Forced to live with a restricted field of vision, I'd developed certain skills to mentally imagine the spatial layout of my environment and map out a course for navigating obstacles without too much difficulty. Yet the extravagant arrangement of this wing's rooms defied all attempts at orientation.

Even by relying on my other senses, it was impossible to determine the uses of these rooms: one was glacially cold, another sweltering hot; one was suffused with a sickly-sweet odour, another reeked of naphthalene; one was sultrily hushed, another resonated with empty echoes; one was bone-dry, another dripped with moisture ...

I'd be hitting my tibias constantly against strangely shaped furniture, my groping hands encountering objects whose edges didn't give me confidence. The headmistress didn't seem too concerned about my poor progress.

"If you start at a slight disadvantage, the game will only be more amusing for the benefactors! The important thing is to make them forget about your eyes. You'll be presented at the next board meeting – provided, of course, that you aren't bleeding."

When I told her that I hadn't yet had my first period, she practically fainted.

"You are so much more than I could hope for, Medusa! If you do me proud, I'll grant you a major privilege: you'll have access to the founder's personal library."

Nothing more was needed to ensure my docility.

When the headmistress had proposed that I become a protégée of the institute, I had assumed that I'd be replacing Suzanne with her adoptive father at the nocturnal parties. I thought that I'd be spending these nights twiddling my thumbs among teddy bears. Yet the shipowner had gone to sea once he'd learned of his daughter's death and had told the board that he wouldn't be back for a year. In the meantime, the other benefactors could try out my play skills.

I hadn't set foot in the boardroom since the night of my arrival. Nonetheless, I recognized the smell of leather and books, the texture of the carpet. My feet trod the same spot where my father had collapsed without causing me any emotion other than a slight irritation.

For my debut, I wore a white, muslin toga that fell to my ankles but left my arms bare. I was entitled to one resin tablet and applied myself to chewing it while the headmistress extolled my merits to the benefactors. To demonstrate my tolerance for pain, she made me hold out my arms straight on each side. She didn't warn me of what would happen.

I felt the owl's talons pierce my skin and dig into my flesh before I even heard it hoot – and understood that I was to serve as its perch. I cried out in surprise, though not in pain: my blindfold exerted enough pressure on my ocular globes to neutralize any discomfort. I let the blood flow from the wounds along my forearm and slowly drip from my fingertips. Every prehensile motion of the owl elicited a languorous moan from me, of which I certainly would've been ashamed if it'd been audible over the squabbling hubbub that had risen in the assembly ...

The benefactors were all so eager to be the first to exploit me that the headmistress had to organize a raffle to determine the order in which they would get to play with me. While she washed my arm and bandaged my wounds, she gave me a last bit of advice:

"Tonight, you'll go before the honourable judge. He's waiting for you in the playroom. I warn you that he can be very stern at times. Whatever happens, don't remove your blindfold. Under any circumstances."

She led me into the wing, pushed me inside a room, and slammed the door behind me.

An imperious, deadwood voice grumbled from the back of the room, ordering me to come forward. I took a few steady steps on the carpet until my toes bumped against an object that shouldn't have been there.

Everything had been moved around in the playroom, depriving me of my reference points. I tried to distinguish through the blindfold any shapes that could help orient me, but my sight still couldn't penetrate the black screen of the knit.

"I was going to suggest we play a game of pichenotte," the judge said in a naturally decisive tone, "but since you're already blindfolded, let's play my version of blind man's bluff."

He handed me a small beam balance, instructing me to hold it up at arm's length while he poured water in each pan. The air in the room was so dry I got an electric shock when I touched the metal.

"You're the living allegory of Blind Justice and must keep the equilibrium of the balance while trying to catch me. For every spilled drop, you'll have to pay a penalty."

He made me turn around three times, and we started the game. I tried to follow the sounds of his stertorous breathing. I was already dazed from the resin and kept getting entangled in the folds of my toga; I was encumbered by the balance and struggled to avoid the obstacles that the judge kept placing in my path in order to increase the game's difficulty.

Put at such a disadvantage, I spilled the pans. The judge's punitive leg shot out from nowhere right in front of me. I couldn't avoid it. I parried the blow by shutting my lids tightly just as I was about to fall, letting myself drop into the void with the abandon of an inert body, my head soothed by the vertigo, my heart borne by the call of gravity. I trembled as the air caressed me and collapsed by the foot of a table as though on a feather mattress. The floor against which my parietal bone crashed was as soft as a pillow.

The judge leaned over my head, not out of concern, but to reprimand me.

"It's a good thing that you don't cry, because I don't tolerate tears. If you tip the balance again, you'll get another kick."

The game started again with a vengeance. Every time I was about to catch the judge, he'd call a penalty and trip me. He never got tired of this little game. The resin helped me maintain a semblance of enthusiasm, but after a few hours, the euphoric effects had faded. My left arm started to weaken, and I switched the balance to the other hand. The judge got angry:

"You're cheating, Medusa! It's a serious infringement of the rules. I wouldn't be just and impartial if I were to show leniency."

He grabbed my index finger, raised it to his mouth, inserted it between his chapped lips, and licked it with his raspy tongue; his spittle was as thick as starch paste. With a sudden manoeuvre, my finger then ended up in a curious, cylindrical metal case, with grooved walls, at the back of which it touched a mammillary protuberance.

Upon contact with it, my finger crackled. An electric discharge shot up my arm with the frenzy of spawning salmon, taking the path of least resistance through my nerves, spreading its piercing quality throughout my body, like hoarfrost branching out on glass.

Time to close my lids with a delicious frisson, my hair standing on end around my head, my breathing choppy, while lewd and inappropriate squeals rose from the back of my throat. The current galvanized my Turpitudes in every fibril of their irises, and I was dazzled from the inside by an apotheosis of light.

Unfortunately, a short circuit abruptly put an end to this moment of pleasure. I reopened my lids and sensed my finger being shoved into the empty socket of a lamp. And I couldn't help noticing that my legs were striped with scrapes and bruises.

I immediately put my hands on my face, sure that I'd lost the blindfold while being punished, yet it was still firmly in place – even slightly tighter. My sight, however, was no longer hampered by its screen. No doubt due to the electric discharge, my Unmentionables now had the ability of seeing through fabric as though it were glass.

All around me, obstacles lay strewn on the floor: a rocking horse, chests stuffed with puppets, spinning tops and mechanical toys, a wooden farm with its miniature animals and stable, a pile of picture books, card tables covered with board games, pawns, dice, puzzles, and dominoes. All set up in a room painted like a nursery in yellow and baby blue.

Thrilled to be able to spy on the judge without him knowing, I turned my attention to him. He was a gnome! Stunted, withered, and wrinkled like tree bark, with a crooked nose and two gold teeth. Age spots riddled his thinning, leathery scalp. As for his eyes – which I was so curious to observe – they'd probably been grey once, but now they were milky-white, clouded by cataracts. His getup was even more surprising: he was dressed like a little boy, in short pants with suspenders and shirt sleeves, and on his feet, white socks and ankle boots. He looked so ridiculous that I was embarrassed for him.

"The other protégées always beg for mercy ... but not you, Medusa. The headmistress didn't lie about you: you really are the ideal playmate. I give you a respite from punishment. Let's be friends, shall we?"

He held out two fingers for me to shake. I don't know how I held back from shoving them into the lamp socket. But I thought of the library, and every seed of rebellion that might have bloomed in me was instantly nipped in the bud.

"I'm granting you a really big favour, Medusa," the headmistress told me as she led me into the boardroom. "No other protégée has ever been invited to see the personal library of the Athenaeum's founder."

Now deceased, the founder apparently had accumulated his fortune thanks to the precious-metal mines he exploited in the northern part of the province. A philanthropist in his spare time, he'd taken up the cause of those most disadvantaged by nature and devoted himself to improving their lot. At his own expense, he had built the institute on one of his many estates and had bequeathed it to a board of thirteen benefactors dedicated to pursuing his charity work.

"The founder was a complex man," the headmistress said with reverence. "Of all his accomplishments, he considered the Athenaeum to be the most commendable and his library the most gratifying."

I scanned the volumes on the mahogany shelves. This library had nothing in common with the hodgepodge of insipid novels found in the study hall. Naturally, it reflected the founder's interest in mineralogy, which extended to geology and astronomy, volcanology, gemology, and cartography ... Above all, it indicated masculine tastes: guides to first aid, wilderness survival, and fly-fishing; monographs on freshwater fish and indigenous plants; general mechanics manuals;

tomes on photography, bridges, and shipwrecks ... which were next to an interesting collection of banned books (illustrated editions of libertine novels, uncensored journals of notorious debauchers, confessions of courtesans, indiscretions of brothel madams), as well as a stack of comics about the adventures of pirates, masked vigilantes, knights, woodwose, time or interstellar travellers, detectives, mythical heroes, mysterious magicians!

In each of these books, I saw a secret door, a satisfied curiosity, a respite from mortal angst. And, of course, a screen for my Demeaningnesses. I finally settled on a thick volume titled *Artistic Forms Found in Nature*, bound in grey cloth, the spine of which featured a white medusa. I reached out my hand to grab it, but it was immediately slapped away.

The headmistress had a totally different work in mind for me, one kept in a glass case with the Athenaeum's precious archives. From a red-leather binding, she pulled out a parchment on which the founder had handwritten a spiritual testament. His writing was full of flourishes, his signature wreathed with curlicues.

"I'll read it out loud to you," the headmistress said with fervour, while her owl flapped its wings in anticipation.

The testament evoked a motley of papal encyclicals, legal texts, political speeches, and esoteric rituals. In bombastic and flowery language, the founder outlined the guiding principles for "this idyllic refuge for young women fated to remain old maids." He urged the benefactors to ensure the survival of this vital institution and reminded them of the importance of protecting its secrets at all costs.

"That's all for today," the headmistress said, putting the testament back. "Tomorrow, I'll read you some of the board meeting minutes."

I looked so utterly disappointed that she couldn't help noticing it.

"Before you can have free access to the books, you must first charm the governor."

While I was training blindfolded, I had imagined the arms room mahoganied like the bookshelves and adorned with symmetrical panoplies – sabres and spears, daggers and morning stars arranged fanlike around huge shields.

Through the weft of the blindfold, I realized my mistake. The room held only projectile weapons that looked like inoffensive toys: slings and slingshots, bows and crossbows for kids, even a miniature catapult. Targets hung on the walls, but they were painted in vibrant colours like an assortment of sorbets. Instead of an odour of iron and copper, the room had a sickly-sweet scent with hints of mint and orange, whose source I couldn't identify.

The governor of the citadel had left the comfort of his official residence and braved the gloomy January weather to honour me with his attentions. He was so hirsute the cold probably didn't bother him. His hairline started low on his brow, his beard went all the way to his eyes, and his eyebrow hair was so rampant it also came out of his nostrils and ears. His body hair was no different, poking out of every opening in his suit. He looked like a real woodsman.

He spoke at length about the citadel's cannons, whose fuses he had lit himself at the New Year's Eve celebrations. His passion for ballistics had no limits,

and he barraged me with facts about propulsion, accel-
eration, and gravity, and the many factors that can
make a shot deviate. I let him talk without interrupting.
I had chewed two resin tablets, and it all seemed almost
interesting to me. I was a bit eager, however, for him
to move away from theory and put his principles into
practice.

At last, the governor unlocked the ammunition case –
and the syrupy perfume flooded the room. The shelves
were lined with candy jars filled with an entire arsenal
of sweets and chocolates: marshmallow bananas, Jolly
Ranchers, liquorice twists, gumballs, cinnamon fish,
pink mints, chocolate coins ... It looked like the inter-
ior of a confectionery shop, or at least its miniature
version.

After he took off his jacket, the governor selected,
from among the weapons at his disposal, a humble
peashooter and aimed it at me, marking the shot with
one eye.

"Excellent!" he exclaimed. "With your blindfold,
you're ready for the firing squad."

From a candy jar, he grabbed a handful of lemon
drops, which he stuffed one by one in his mouth. He
sucked them noisily and rolled them between his teeth,
keeping me in his sightline.

My face was soon bombarded by acidic hailstones,
which made my nose bleed. As soon as I closed my
lids, however, the pain subsided, and I let the lozenges
stream down on me like a summer rainstorm.

"A bit too easy," the governor said, exchanging the
peashooter for a slingshot. "Now walk up and down

like one of those mechanical targets in a shooting range at a fairground."

This time around, he used berlingots, pralines, and barley sugars as projectiles, which kneaded my flesh like the skilled hands of a masseur, since the governor was a sharp shooter: he hit the nail on the head every time. When he wanted to show me that his expertise extended to the bow and crossbow, he chose pointy lollipops. He reserved the Turkish delights and jujubes for the catapult.

By the end of the night, my skin was sticky, my hair glazed in sugar, and I couldn't wait to go wash myself. But the governor still intended to deliver his coup de grâce.

"Now, open your mouth wide and don't move!" he said, backing up ten steps or so. "I'm going to attempt the feat that only a true marksman can do."

He unwrapped a caramel and after chewing it for a long time, expelled it with force along with some tobacco-coloured spit. I saw the projectile make a perfect arc as it came down towards me, crossing my lips like an arrow to land directly at the back of my throat.

I tried to spit out the caramel but only managed to choke on it. The air wasn't passing through, and I really thought that I was going to suffocate. Just as a black veil started descending over my Screwballs, the governor gave me a big slap on the back, the caramel got dislodged, and I could breathe again.

"You're the perfect target, Medusa!" he said, snapping his suspenders. "You must admit you're impressed."

I left the arms room sweeping all the candies I was likely to slip on out of the way with my foot. As for that damn caramel, I can assure you that its memory is still stuck in my throat.

The next day, I was woken by the rhythmic cadence of hammering coming from the headmistress's rooms. I found her on her knees in the middle of her boudoir, in front of a large travel trunk, whose lock she was trying to force open. Her not-so-vigorous blows were having no effect on the shackle, which didn't even budge an inch.

"Sorry about the noise, Medusa, but I can't remember where I put the key for this trunk. Actually, I might've tossed it into the lake ... I never thought I'd need it again."

She handed me the hammer and pliers. The shackle was rusted; it gave way with a percussive bang, the lid swung open, and a confusion of fabrics, lace, and ribbons spilled out, dissipating particles of dust and spores of mould in the air.

The headmistress started riffling through the pile of threadbare rags with the emotion of some great rediscovery. I'd never seen her so animated. She unfolded a bodice, shook out a skirt, and dreamily admired them before setting them on the carpet beside her.

The trunk held a wide assortment of disparate outfits: a Columbine costume whose colourful diamonds were sadly faded; a princess dress with the hems coming undone; a ballerina leotard and a pink, frayed tutu so washed out it looked bled dry; a hospital gown made of yellowed, brittle linen; a grass-green sheath dress of worn-out velvet; an apron with pockets full of holes; an oriental robe with a missing belt; petticoats, camisoles, crinolines ...

"I used to wear costumes when I was still young enough to amuse the benefactors," the headmistress said, continuing to rummage nostalgically in the trunk.

I was not surprised to learn that she was a former protégée of the institute, nor that she had been the very first. However, I didn't expect what she revealed next, in the greatest of confidence.

"I had this privilege because I was the daughter of the mining magnate," she confided with solemnity, bursting with pride. "You see, my father was the founder of the Athenaeum."

The headmistress had been born with a very sparse head of hair and scant eyelashes and eyebrows. Her congenital alopecia also affected the rest of her body. By puberty, she'd lost her scarce body hair and her thinning tresses started falling out in clumps.

"There's nothing more terrible for a young girl than being deprived of one of the most glorious attributes of femininity," she said, running her fingers lightly over my blindfold. "You know what that's like, don't you?"

With her bald cranium, plucked brow, and naked eyelids, the daughter of the mining magnate couldn't have been anything but a source of shame for an eminent family such as hers. It's not surprising that her father wanted to put some distance between himself and his disgraceful offspring and remove from his lineage any suggestion of possible inbreeding, corruption of his seed, and degeneration of his line.

He could've sent his daughter to a convent, but he was a freethinker and anticlerical and refused to see his daughter, defective though she may be, join any kind of order. In truth, he didn't know what else to do. He didn't necessarily renounce her – at least not entirely … He banished her to the shores of this isolated lake, on this estate safe from prying eyes and which he visited just once a year.

It was his personal playground and he invited no one besides his former schoolmates from the Catholic boys' school. Their friendship had been cemented by a cloistered childhood spent in boarding school, confined to study, reduced to silence, and repressed by the strict authority of discipline masters. Within the grounds and wilderness of the estate, they could reconnect with their childishness, make up for lost shenanigans, and freely give in to all the infantile behaviour that was once forbidden to them.

"My father was kind enough to give me asylum in his retreat. He offered me protection against the world's cruelty and did me the great favour of not cutting me off from his presence – even though I had to keep to my room whenever he visited the estate."

With an old servant as her sole companion, the young girl had found the long winter months, far from her family, very tedious. As soon as spring would arrive, however, she would leave the estate and go exploring in the forest. Accompanied by the screeching of squirrels and the warbling of robins, she'd gather ferns and lady's slippers and make crowns to hide her baldness.

It was during one of these outings that she discovered, at the foot of a hollowed ash, an owl chick who had fallen from the nest. She picked it up, nestled it in a pillow's feathers, fed it sugar water with an eyedropper, then small pieces of various prey – plump shrews and fat bullfrogs – that she caught herself. The owl allowed itself to be tamed and found, on the gloved hand of its mistress, a natural perch.

One day, the headmistress was lingering by the lakeshore, braiding herself a wig of weeds, when she was surprised by her father. The mining magnate was surrounded by his cronies – a gang of jolly fellows in walking shoes, tweed jackets, and breeches. They didn't hesitate to stare at the tall, bald girl, then started whistling in a manner that was in no way complimentary.

"I'd forgotten that my father was supposed to arrive that day," the headmistress went on. "I thought that he wouldn't forgive my transgression and, despite his reticence, would pack me off to a convent immediately. I sorely underestimated his magnanimity."

Instead of getting angry, the magnate grabbed a handful of stringy algae and deposited it on his daughter's head to complete the wig. Then he picked up two black caterpillars from the cattails and made her two slithering eyebrows. The joke was met with unanimous approval.

His companions didn't leave it at that. They made the young girl suffer a series of cruelties and humiliations, harassment and detainment, bullying and oppression inspired by the hazing rituals that have been perpetuated in colleges for centuries and that assure the indissoluble cohesion of fraternities. The victim was tossed into the lake though she didn't know how to swim, rolled around in the mud, pushed into the embers of a campfire, forced to swallow a beetle, kiss a garter snake, and smoke a cigar until she was sick.

"I was thrilled to be the centre of so much attention at last," the headmistress said in an elated voice. "It was the most important day of my life. I came out of this initiation even more devoted to my father than before and ready to dedicate myself to serving his friends."

For the former schoolmates, this pleasurable episode also proved to be a revelation. Raised apart from girls, they had never known the joy of tormenting them, pulling their hair, lifting up their skirts, tripping them, throwing snowballs at them, locking them in closets, or tying them to trees. And they certainly couldn't engage in such activities with their wives or daughters.

This is how the headmistress became their designated playmate, that is to say their ball, their dice, their pawn. She remained so for five years, which, according to her, were the best years of her life. She abided by the rules, followed instructions, accepted the most arbitrary decisions, submitted to penalties, sought their approval, fervently hoped for their compliments. However, the demands of the playfellows increasingly stretched the limits of her endurance, and her cries would often interrupt the games.

"I would've given everything to have your

insensitivity to pain," she said, adjusting a lock of my hair. "Then I would've remained the exclusive companion of the benefactors ... But this idyllic state came to a brutal end one day when my father announced that I was too old to play with them and that, in any case, I no longer amused them."

To replace her, the founder had the idea of finding thirteen new playmates from among girls with congenital deformities languishing in orphanages and adopting them, so as to have full rights over them. At great expense, he transformed the estate into an institute dedicated to the education of the protégées and, in his generosity, allocated an entire wing to amusement.

"As you know, Medusa, the owl is the symbol of the goddess Athena, and my owl was my father's inspiration for the institute's name. He also had the aviary made especially for her – an honour that reflected on me."

The founder was once again indulgent enough to keep his daughter close to him and placed her in charge of the boarders' education – a task she accepted with gratitude and carried out with the utmost diligence. She welcomed the poor girls, got them accustomed to the place, instilled discipline in them, and prepared them for the games.

"My father counted on me to train the protégées like I'd trained my owl. I was full of pride at the great trust he had placed in me. I would've done anything not to let him down."

In her blind fervour, she was in no way troubled by the memory of all the boarders she had forever silenced simply to ensure that the benefactors' activities would never be disclosed. The pain of being scrapped, however, still stung. She held a grudge against the protégées who had replaced her. She'd watch them go into the benefactors' wing with envy and would console herself with resin.

With a sigh, she went back to riffling through the trunk, extracted a lab coat, and placed it before me.

"Here, I have a present for you. You'll wear it to meet your next playmate: the king of rye. He owns the largest distillery in the city."

When the founder had redeveloped the estate, he'd built a bar with well-stocked shelves in the private wing. The king of rye had made it his lair.

When I entered, a cupel was heating up over a Bunsen burner and a nauseating smoke was emanating from a residue of burnt powder. On the counter, between various glasses and bottles of spirits, was an entire array of test tubes, pipettes, and beakers filled with unidentifiable liquids.

"Welcome to my lab of smoke and mirrors!" the distiller said, bursting into jovial chuckles.

The man was rotund, blondish, and curly-haired with a complexion striated by a tenacious, crimson vermiculation. He invited me to sit on a stool – and just as I was about to sit, suddenly pulled it out from under me. I fell straight on my posterior, clanging my coccyx. The little prankster laughed so hard he practically dislocated his jaw, and I was treated to a low-angle shot of his uvula, tonsils, and all the fillings in his upper molars – as well as a reeking waft of his alcoholic breath, strong enough to curdle milk. Without helping me get up, he walked behind the counter and started pouring various liquids into test tubes.

"Don't take off your blindfold, because I'm mixing an expert concoction and you're going to guess its secret ingredients."

With my face still red with confusion, I sat down again, only to discover that the distiller had padded the stools with whoopee cushions. Wiping away tears of laughter, he stirred his brew with a glass rod; it turned a purplish maroon. He then poured it into a wineglass, smacking his lips with satisfaction.

I closed my Brazenitudes before bringing it to my lips. I recognized the taste of vinegar, anchovy paste, bleach, cod-liver oil, violet-scented soap, and borax. The mad scientist was thrilled that his rotgut brought no tears to my eyes, and he made me drink his other inventions all night long. I was subjected to itching powder, stink bombs, flour fireballs, sneezing powder, chili-pepper candy, dirty soap, sugar laxatives. I endured all these humiliations with a straight face.

As soon as I was back in my room, my stomach revolted and I puked my guts out. As you can see, the king of rye's laughter had remained stuck in my throat, and I've never digested it.

On the recommendation of the benefactors I had met, the headmistress finally allowed me to be alone in the boardroom. During the blissful hours I spent there without her supervision, I had ample opportunity to consult the archives of the Athenaeum – and riffle through the files within files of its many secrets. I have them on hand and could copy out entire passages for you. But I'd rather avoid this drudgery and spare you the tedium of reading them.

Just know that the archives go all the way back to the opening of the institute and cover a period of some thirty years. They conserve the financial statements of the foundation, the minutes (meticulously recorded by the headmistress) of the board meetings, the rules governing membership dues, the dress code, a large accounting book listing all expenses, including the repair costs for the playroom, the smoking room, the exercise room, the music room, the laboratory, the arms room, the woodshop, the observatory, the winter garden, the infirmary, the water room, the banquet hall, and the resting room.

A binder holds about forty reports on all the protégées who had the misfortune to be admitted to the Athenaeum, listing their name, place of origin, and age at arrival. Medical records attest to sad fates and lives condemned by some congenital defect: facial malformations, port-wine stains, strabismus, gibbosity, kyphosis, congenital dislocations, cleft palate, varus deformities, malformed ears, umbilical hernia, syndactyly, nasal agenesis, macroglossia, axial hypotonia, acromegaly …

From among the protégées rejected because of age or because they'd fallen out of favour, the headmistress had recruited eleven matrons. As for the others, she'd disposed of them in such a way that the benefactors' secrets would never come to light. In their files, the date of their departure is the only funerary inscription that these poor girls ever received.

Over the years, several benefactors passed away or retired due to health reasons; the board found replacements for them from among important personages in our city in order to maintain a quorum of thirteen members. Besides the governor, the judge, and the distillery king, their members included the owner of the coliseum, the hospital director, the zookeeper, the bandmaster, the superintendent of roads and bridges, the regional press baron, our national poet, the bank treasurer, the president of the chamber of commerce, as well as the most prosperous shipowner of our merchant fleet. All had made substantial donations to the foundation.

The archives preserve a parchment signed by the conspirators in their own blood, in which they swear to never reveal anything about what goes on within the Athenaeum's walls, under penalty of death. They are bound by a double bloody secret: that of their shame and that of their murderous culpability.

These alleged freethinkers refuse to follow any dogma lacking a scientific or philosophical foundation, yet they abide by the archaic rules of their secret society. They call themselves enlightened, yet they keep their protégées in the most abject ignorance. They think themselves free, yet they are slaves to their puerile passions.

If you want to really know what I think, I find their hypocrisy a thousand times more monstrous than the deformities of their protégées.

The benefactors had a dedicated protégée, yet they shared their adopted daughters between them with prodigious frequency. Their evaluations of each girl's recreational aptitudes are all preserved in the archives.

There's also a file on me, packed full of laudatory quotes. According to my evaluators, I didn't always fully abide by the rules; however, when I'd lose, I'd submit to the penalties graciously and ask for a rematch in an appropriate infantile voice ...

It's true that I assimilated the rules very quickly. I'd mould myself into the role that the benefactors expected of me, anticipating their desires, embodying their ideal playmate – which was not all that difficult given the limitations of their imaginations and the predictability of their challenges.

They each had their reserved areas, their assigned toys, their particular demands. Their favourite games not only revealed their nature, character, manias, and obsessions, but also their easily offended vanities.

Our regional press baron, for example, was an inveterate cheater. When we would play hide-and-seek in the observatory, he'd spy on me through a periscope, telescope, or binoculars while counting to ten. He'd have no trouble finding me and, to celebrate his victory, he'd pull my hair hard enough to rip it out.

Our national poet would stage sketches on the small

podium in the banquet hall and, dressed up as a musketeer, cowboy, or fireman, ask me to solve riddles or play charades. Then he'd launch into a tirade of puerile jokes and, to make sure I laughed, tickle me mercilessly with his clammy hand, scratching my neck, prickling my sides, irritating my stomach until I'd lose control of my bladder.

The owner of the coliseum had installed all sorts of playground equipment in the exercise room: a swing, a seesaw, a roundabout, monkey bars, stilts ... He was proud of his physical fitness and the feats he could accomplish hands-free. If I didn't applaud his somersaults, he'd twist my arm behind my back and make me repeat that he was the strongest, the most agile, the fastest, the handsomest.

As for the bank treasurer, he couldn't get enough of demonstrating his dexterity with the cup-and-ball, the paddleball, and the yo-yo. Every time he missed, he'd get furious and, with all the force of his frustrated pride, he'd throw jacks and marbles at me, calling me names.

The strict duties of their offices must have weighed heavily on the benefactors for them to feel the need to periodically engage in childish behaviour not appropriate for their age. But who can say why they felt compelled to exercise their malice through a thousand and one cruelties? What did thumbing their noses, sticking out their tongues and making faces, jeering, taunting, and name-calling, ridiculing and mocking my flaws do for them?

They were far from young and handsome. You didn't need my sharp vision to see that they were disfigured by wrinkles, blackheads, craterous pores, cysts, chapped skin, rosacea, atrophic scars, ingrown hairs, age spots, warts. Could they not see what they were when they looked in the mirror?

The resin may have made their abuse bearable, but their unforgivable insults have remained etched in my memory as though in stone.

My musical literacy is, I admit, a great gaping hole. However, I know the approximate composition of a concert band: I learned it at the expense of my poor eardrums when I spent the night in the music room.

Don't imagine a hushed room fitted with soundproofing panels and velvet curtains. The room was bare to amplify the echo effect. The array of instruments included a trumpet, cymbals, a flageolet, a bass drum, a triangle, maracas, a trombone, a clarinet, a xylophone, a glockenspiel ... However, these woodwind, brass, and percussion instruments were toy versions made of plastic and painted metal. Their adorable size and vibrant colours did not, I assure you, in any way diminish their unbearable, strident shrill.

"Here you are at last!" the bandmaster exclaimed, brandishing his baton. "Now the concert can begin!"

The man had the thundering voice of someone over-compensating for a hearing problem; his hair, greased back to bare his sharp forehead, looked like the erectile crest of a hoopoe. His idea of a concert was to make the greatest racket possible. He grated my ears by comparing the decibel power of a tambourine with that of a bell rattle. He interpreted children's songs from his vast repertoire on the kazoo.

Then we played musical chairs while beating drums,

merry-go-round while clicking castanets, jack-in-the-box while tooting a flageolet ...

This musical carousel lasted hours. The bandmaster worked himself up into a devilish frenzy, overexcited by the deafening effect of his cacophony. Unfortunately, the resin didn't help me in the slightest. As if I hadn't endured enough already, I heard the discordant sound of an accordion and the stentor's voice bark this demeaning command: "Turn, my little spinning top!"

Already dizzy from going round and round, I tried to spin. As soon as I did, I felt a ripple in my head, and the blood rushing to my brain made me feel so nauseous I feared the resin would come back out. My legs twisted, my feet got all tangled up, and I fell over.

The bandmaster applauded. He had no intention of letting me regain my balance, however. He sat down on a stool in front of a glockenspiel with metal plates painted in rainbow colours. Smoothing his hair back to right his crest and gazing towards the ceiling, he suddenly seemed struck by inspiration and began playing a crude three-note tune, repeating it over and over.

"Now turn like a ballerina in a music box!"

This time, I shut my lids hermetically before making a few pirouettes. The dizziness didn't diminish, but at least it seemed more tolerable ... and less disagreeable. The nausea dissipated, and the vertigo became exhilarating. Intoxicated by the floating sensation that accompanied it, I barely noticed that the exasperating ditty had metamorphosed into a lullaby. New notes built on other notes, forming chords, arpeggios, variations, modulations ...

Abruptly, the bandmaster reached the finale and stood up with a victorious cry.

"I've always dreamed of composing a lullaby for music boxes," he admitted, wiping his bluff-like brow. "Until now, I'd only been able to find the first notes ... You are a muse, Medusa!"

He complemented my endurance and the perfection of my tempo. He told me that I could stop spinning now. But I no longer heard him. I was caught up in a hypnotic vortex, like the medusae in the whirlpool of the lake. Subject to the centrifugal force of my spinning, my hair pirouetted like whizzing arrows. I almost lost my blindfold and felt like I was about to fly away. Far from the bandmaster. And far from the institute.

Lacking a brain or central nervous system, medusae must nonetheless feel dazed when caught in the eddies of the lake. Like all cnidarians, they have a hem of sensory cells on the edge of their bells that not only help them to maintain their balance and orient themselves in space, but also to sense the water's luminosity, analyze chemical compositions, detect smells, assess the temperature – and feel contact with their prey.

They get their name from Medusa because of their analogous shape to the Gorgon's head of serpents. Did you know that in periods of famine, they can sometimes eat their own gonads? I learned this in a monograph on medusae that I found in the founder's library. The book includes forty illustrations painted by a German naturalist named Haeckel, who was the first to successfully document (by enlarging them under a microscope) the different morphologies and cells of these ephemeral animals. Composed almost entirely of gelatinous water, they leave behind no bones, scales, or fossils, but only a thin film, as fine as a sheet of bible paper.

Executed in white chalk on blue paper, the illustrations depict, in profile and cross-section, the bells, oral arms, tentacles, and mouth cavities. A few more detailed watercolours of the seabed show medusae swimming in their natural habitat.

However, most of the images simply elaborate the

many shapes that medusae can have. In them, you can recognize architectural ornamentation, crystal chandeliers, coats of arms, Abyssinian corals, ribbons of lace, bridal veils, star rays, aspic moulds, fringed lampshades, mushrooms with twisted roots, feather plumes, frilly hats, parachutes, spiderwebs, eyeballs with the optic nerve dragging behind them, as well as a wide variety of genital organs ...

The fact is that you'd never suspect medusae to be venomous. You see, even the most fragile beauty can be monstrous.

The winter garden, located at the end of the benefactors' wing, is not, strictly speaking, a garden. Yes, it houses an abundance of ferns and glossy-leafed tropical plants under the rosy glow of fluorescent lights. However, the vegetation is imprisoned behind the glass of large vivaria and serves as a nest to toads, spiders, scutigera, scolopendra, earthworms, and garter snakes. At the centre of the greenhouse, a pool of water smothered in water lilies holds frogs, salamanders and their efts, and various other creepy-crawlies captured by the zookeeper on his walks in the area.

"At the zoo, we house only exotic animals," he said in a monotonous voice by way of greeting me. "Our lakes and forests, however, abound with very interesting myriapods, millipedes, annelids, reptiles, and amphibians."

He told me the Latin names of each of his specimens, described their anatomy, detailed their behaviour and modes of reproduction without dislodging his nose from a vivarium where a handful of garter snakes (ten females and one male) formed what is called a mating ball.

I thought I had nothing to fear from this man with soft features and a weak chin. Behind his jam-jar glasses, his shifty eyes were duller than lead. His gestures were sluggish and prone to hesitation.

He became more animated only once he'd extracted

a dice from his pocket. He pointed out that the colourful slate tiles on the ground formed a checkerboard pattern. We then played his version of snakes and ladders.

Every time a toss of the dice made me land on a green tile, the zookeeper would fish out an earthworm or centipede from one of the vivaria and drop it down my back, between my nape and collar; if I landed on a red tile, he'd slip a garter snake or leech down the slit of my bodice.

In no time, I was jacketed in creepy-crawlies, covered in stings and bites. Without the resin, I would never have been able to overcome the disgust I felt at the slithering legs, clammy metameres, and scales crawling all over my stomach. I was so stupefied, however, that I willingly offered my epidermis to their indecent explorations. With my lids half shut under the blindfold, which had loosened up a bit, I sampled these new sensations with an alert curiosity.

I'd landed on a red tile and was waiting for the penalty. The zookeeper was frozen in indecision until he noticed the knot of green garter snakes. He placed it on my head like a crown. The snakes immediately separated and started twisting into my hair, and one of them (the male, no doubt) took shelter under my blindfold. Upon contact with its icy scales, my Degradingnities were transfixed with ecstasy and unabashedly quivered with orgasmic pleasure.

When I reopened my lids, my gaze fell on the shadow that I projected onto the slate tiles: a long silhouette crowned with serpents. Medusa's shadow.

With hindsight, I regret so meekly consenting to these dangerous games with merciless men who couldn't be trusted and from whom I could never hope to have any affection.

But you need to understand that after spending a childhood bored with my own company, I finally had a chance to have playmates. While the resin kept me in languorous amorality, I was also discovering the many configurations of games, the particularities of chance, the thrill of competition, the abandonment of laughter … My wonder helped me withstand the injustice and perversity of the rules.

What disturbed me more was the physical pleasure I experienced from these physical cruelties. I would welcome with open arms the primitive instincts of my Obscenities, their unbridled sensuality and base inclinations. The next day, however, I'd be awakened by the bugle call of their memory and, reeling from shame, bury my face in the pillow. I was horrified at myself.

So I must stuff my face full of resin tablets before I can admit to you the tremors that shook me to the marrow when the hospital director – the doctor who had pronounced my father's death – received me in the woodshop and shackled me to a game of Meccano. Assembling metal razor blades, angle bars, brass axles, and gears with screws and wingnuts, he built me a custom-fit corset, a sheath, splints, elbow orthoses, ankle braces, and a helmet. As per his instructions, I then walked around the room like a robot and, with every jerky step, let the razor blades impale me from all sides.

I could also tell you about the feverishness that flared up in me in the torrid humidity of the water room where the president of the chamber of commerce, dressed up as a pirate, at last abandoned the little sailboats he was splashing around in the bathtub and started tying me up in a variety of uncomfortable positions that challenged my flexibility, making use of his vast repertoire of sailing knots: the clove hitch, the carrick bend, the common whipping, the half hitch, the rat-tail stopper, the sheepshank, the alpine butterfly, the Portuguese bowline, the cat's paw, the cow hitch, the slip knot, the anchor bend, the surgeon's loop, the scaffold …

He challenged me to try to get myself loose, but I had to give up: every time I made the smallest movement, the knots would get even tighter. Contortioned on the marble tiles, I savoured the pressure on my ankles and wrists, the unfamiliar straining of my muscles, the constriction of my joints, the pins and needles in my extremities deprived of circulation. I remained immobile in this vulnerable numbness until the ropes cut into my skin and my blood trickled into the puddles of water.

I'd had enough of dulling my senses with resin, so when I was summoned to the smoking room to meet the superintendent of roads and bridges, I spat the tablets out.

The cigar cases and matchboxes held a collection of miniature cars in vibrant colours and shiny chrome, which almost made you forget the nicotine-stained walls, the sour, ashtray stench of the carpets, the nauseating smoke-filled air, and the tobacco spittle the superintendent spluttered.

I didn't appreciate being transformed into a racetrack when he made me stretch out on the floor and placed foam trees and bushes, miniature houses, fences, bridges, and other elements of a model landscape on my body.

Blithely sucking on a cigar he held in the corner of his mouth, he started imitating a rumbling engine by making his thick lips vibrate, while cars climbed up my hills, raced down my valleys, circumvented sudden roadside accidents, crossed and recrossed bridges ...

Any tiny movement on my part threatened to unleash an earthquake that would've devastated the terrain and pitched the tiny cars into the landscape. No splints or ropes bound me this time. I was no less paralyzed, however, because the superintendent blocked my nose and mouth to keep me from breathing ...

My lungs became rigid, my heart slowed down, my pupils dilated. In the revealing euphoria of asphyxiation, I saw myself as a corpse. I became aware of the passive role that was paralyzing me and the profound dissatisfaction that these recreational activities instilled in me.

I wanted to become mistress of the game, and the only amusement I could've enjoyed at that moment would've been to tear off my blindfold and scare the superintendent.

The shame of showing my Terrors held my hand back, of course. Deep down, I hadn't yet accepted that I was a monster.

Thirty new moons had passed since I'd entered into the benefactors' service, and I hadn't yet met the shipowner. He hadn't been heard of since Suzanne had died. As he was the one who supplied the institute with resin, his prolonged absence had gotten the headmistress all in a fluster, since the supply had almost run out.

At last, he was back in the country and the accolades his benefactor friends bestowed on my person finally piqued his curiosity. He was eager to meet me and promised to come to the next nocturnal party.

The headmistress rushed to tell me of his arrival while I was in the boardroom, stretched out on the window seat and captivated by the story of the infamous shipwreck of the frigate *Méduse* off the coast of Mauritania. It was my favourite reading nook: looking out over the forest, seeing it change from season to season, I could almost forget where I was.

She stuck her bald head through the half-open door and was surprised to see me reading with the blindfold over my eyes. I'd forgotten to raise it and had to confess that I could see through it very easily. Her puzzled expression changed to a smile.

"Well that just makes things so much simpler, Medusa, since I have big plans for us."

She came and sat by me on the window seat – an ominous sign that she was about to take me into her confidence.

"When the founder died, the benefactors had the kindness to grant me the stewardship of the institute, and I have jealously safeguarded the paternal legacy," she said in a solemn voice. "My mission now is to ensure its long-term survival. It's not too early to begin training my successor."

Then she caressed my cheek.

"You have a great future among us, Medusa. After the benefactors release you, I'll enlist you as one of the matrons. You'll be in charge of training the protégées and teaching them endurance. Then, one day, I will pass you the torch and you will direct the Athenaeum!"

I considered the prospect of this tantalizing future and wondered if it wouldn't be better, after all, to be tossed into the lake with my hands and feet bound …

What refuge is there for monsters like me? The centre of a labyrinth? A bunker beneath a lake? A castle in the Carpathians? An infernal abyss? Medusa had been able to escape to the ends of the earth on a rocky island where the poor wretches who dared venture there would be turned to stone. But I didn't have that luxury. For me, the institute was the thing that most resembled a remote island.

The ship owner had the cosmopolitan flair, casual ease, and tanned skin of the frequent traveller. He was one of those showy fops with a dull brow, flat nose, and features too symmetrical to stir up emotion. Vainly careful about his appearance, he was clean-shaven, powdered and pomaded with moderation, and his nails were impeccably buffed.

I must admit that he looked quite elegant in his flannel, dinosaur-patterned pyjamas, and that he cut a fine figure standing in the middle of the resting room, leaning on a Malacca cane, a mountain of stuffed animals at his feet.

"My ship was the first to reach port this year, and they gave me this little toy," he told me, stroking the gold handle of the cane with his fingertips, as though checking for scratches.

He was younger than the other benefactors and the last one to join their circle. As a seaman who wanted no attachments, he'd never married. His adoption of Suzanne, an agreement he'd signed rashly, had been just an impure formality. There was nothing in his attitude to suggest that he was the least bit troubled by her death.

Suzanne's short stature had surely been ideal for pillow fighting and jumping on the daybed in the alcove, but I was far from having her scaled-down dimensions.

I thought the shipowner would be annoyed, but he was quite pleased that I almost reached his height. He brought his face closer to mine.

"The headmistress assured me that you can see through the blindfold. I certainly want to believe it, but I need proof. Do you know the mirror game? You must imitate the opposite of every gesture I make. So don't let me out of your sight!"

First he took a few poses, stood on his hands, did some rolls and somersaults. Squinting, I focussed my gaze on him: my Afflictions managed to break down his movements and I reproduced them faithfully. He couldn't get enough of admiring the reflection I was sending back to him and stopped only when he was overcome by a yawning fit.

"Your gaze is more attentive than that of the other girls," he said, grabbing a teddy bear by the paw. "Even through your blindfold, I feel its intensity and it gives me goosebumps ... My benefactor friends didn't lie when they swore that you were the ideal playmate. Now, it's time for beddy-byes, and you're going to watch over my sleep."

I first had to pour him a glass of water, tuck him into a blanket patterned with rockets, tell him a story, sing him a lullaby, and turn on the night light. Seated at the foot of the daybed, I focussed my gaze on his eyelids, and he fell asleep in no time, sucking his thumb with the teddy in his arms.

He woke up an hour later, well rested. He went to get dressed behind the screen, in a very excitable state.

"I suffer from insomnia and can never get any rest.

But your eyes rocked me to sleep like the waves. Truly, you're much too precious to remain locked up in here, Medusa. Come with me, and I'll show you the world!"

I reminded the shipowner that the benefactors, let alone the headmistress, would never allow me to leave the institute.

"Then let me steal you away while they're still occupied with the other protégées. By the time they leave tomorrow, we'll have already set sail."

Given the position I was in, how could I have ever refused such a proposal? I didn't even stop to wonder what kind of man the shipowner might be or what kind of life awaited me on his cargo ship. I followed him blindly.

Exiting the institute, we passed by the aviary. I didn't give the owl any time to alert the headmistress of our escape. I took off my blindfold, and my Agonies swooped down on its yellow eyes. The owl's cry died in mid-air, its body stiffened, and it crashed to the ground like stone.

Before putting my blindfold back on, I turned towards the lake and bid my goodbyes to Suzanne.

In the car that was taking me far from the institute, the shipowner said, "From now on, I'll be your guardian. And you'll be my pupil."

When we reached the seaway, a cargo ship chartered to transport grain was waiting for us in the shipyard, ready to cast off. Before boarding, however, the ship-owner took me down a shadowy lane leading to the harbour.

"You can't keep going around with a blindfold," he announced, stopping in front of a sign shaped like a monocle. He pushed the door open and, ducking his head to avoid knocking his brow against the frame, walked into the dark shop ahead of me.

An old spectacle maker was bent over his work-bench, busy polishing a lens. A cat lurking at his feet turned a few circles around itself and hissed at me before running off. A dusty display case held several tortoiseshell, metal, and horn-rimmed spectacles that all had black, opaque lenses: the optician made glasses for the blind.

The shipowner explained that he was looking for a model that would cover my eyes entirely without dis-figuring my face.

"Glasses worthy of my pupil, whatever the price."

Hearing these words, the optician, who hadn't left his workbench, hastened towards me and asked me to remove my blindfold. I kept my lids shut while he took various measurements with his millimetric ruler.

"I have just what you need," he said, opening the display case.

From a battered glasses case, he took out a pair of glasses so fancy they seemed completely incongruous in the setting. The fine, filigree frame was gold. The lenses, shaped like walnut shells, were made of one-way glass; the exterior side was reflective, while the interior, transparent side allowed a person to see without being seen.

"A real gem," the optician emphasized to the ship-owner. "They were ordered by a somewhat eccentric old dowager who pretended to be blind so she could spy on people. The poor woman died before she could take possession."

With a great deal of care, he fitted the glasses on my nose, made a few modifications to the bridge, and adjusted the temple tips behind my ears. Like an eye bath, the glass shells fit the morphology of my face so well that not a single ray of light filtered through. I ran no risk, therefore, of inadvertently exposing my Cyclones.

I could've never imagined that a simple pair of glasses would transform my perspective to such an extent. I now had a shield that not only protected others from my Abjections, but also helped me to face the world about which I knew almost nothing – and which still intimidated me.

Leaving the optician's workshop, I plucked up the courage to raise my head, straighten my neck and right my shoulders, free my face from the cocoon of my hair, expose my cheeks to the sun and wind. I saw the sky, the clouds, the treetops. I watched birds flying over rooftops ... until the shipowner brought me to heel.

"You're my pupil, which means that your pupils belong to me from now on. Make sure that they never look away from my person."

We settled into the most spacious stateroom – a suite reserved, in seafaring tradition, for the shipowner. The opulent decor, in lacquered rosewood, of the living room, bedroom, and bathroom was fit for a transatlantic liner. In anticipation of storms, the furniture was screwed to the walls, the books were protected by recessed shelves, and the armchairs were bolted to the floor and fitted with straps.

My guardian promised that he would buy me a new wardrobe at the next port of call, since I had nothing but the dress on my back. In the meantime, he picked out, from among his neatly arranged silk shirts, suits, and dressing gowns in the closets, an assortment of outfits about my size. What did I care about dressing as a man, since I never looked at myself in the mirror?

It was in this stateroom that I would be confined for the duration of the crossing: in fact, the shipowner had no intention of sharing my attention with the rest of the crew.

First, I would attend to the elaborate ritual of his washing and dressing, then follow his every gesture as he went about his petty occupations. In the afternoons, he'd sit at his desk and read technical and financial reports, journals of port terminals and maritime law.

My Delinquencies would sometimes try to deceive the shipowner's vigilance: under the cover of the one-way glasses, they'd sneak up to the porthole and take off towards the sea, the sky, the horizon ...

My guardian had his suspicions, so to test my diligence, he'd make me play the mirror game. He'd draw my attention back to him constantly by making signs, snapping his fingers, hailing me, and calling me to order.

After one week, I knew him by heart and from every angle.

I had become his captive spectator, his shadow, his pale reflection.

One evening, as the vessel was nearing the shore, the shipowner was called to the deck.

"I'll be gone an hour, don't leave this room," he said.

I hadn't stepped foot outside the stateroom since the day we'd left; I was certainly not going to miss the opportunity of taking in the sea air. I grabbed the first coat I could see and went out.

I almost got lost in the maze of narrow passageways and spartan-grey stairwells, whose only landmarks were a tangle of pipes, valves, and cables oozing rust. At last I came out on the aft deck, which was constellated with residue spat out by the smokestack. The engine fan made an infernal racket. As for the famous sea air, it was saturated with fuel oil.

With my elbows resting on the railing and hair blowing in the wind, I contemplated the reflection of the stars in the sea's black water. Their twinkling seemed to be pulsating towards me. Intrigued, I took off my glasses and saw a constellation of luminescent creatures borne by the current clustering around the hull. In their bodies haloed by thousands of vermillion tentacles, I recognized the lion's mane jellyfish, which is one of the largest and most venomous of the species. They were in the middle of a mating dance.

The gathers of their bells were rhythmically swaying,

trailing behind their cotillions an insatiable torrent of ribbons and lace. The males expelled milky clouds of semen from their mouths that the females then sucked into their stomachs, which hold the eggs. Some of the medusae fought each other with their oral arms, and I must confess to you that this aggressive frenzy dazzled me as much as their reproductive frolicking: it seemed as though in it I was discovering all the ocean's mysteries and the origins of the world.

At the same time, I felt a visceral pity seeing the medusae so encumbered by their manes, subject to the tossing waves, limited in their sensory perception, despised for their intangible appearance and lethal sting. In them I recognized damned souls, I guess.

While leaning further over the railing, I sensed a sly presence creep up behind me. Before I could turn around, two hands bore down on my Calamities.

"Peekaboo, guess who!" said a slimy voice that didn't belong to the shipowner.

Can you imagine how infuriated I felt by this inappropriate fondling of the most intimate part of my anatomy? My modesty was shaken to the core.

I struggled to get free, but the intruder was crushing my lids with all his might.

"Your fingers are greasy and you smell of burnt fat, so you must be the ship's cook," I said.

This insult dampened his enthusiasm somewhat.

"And you're the shipowner's ward. Would you like to know my pedigree?"

I didn't particularly, but without waiting for my answer, he started emphatically enumerating the list of crowned heads and eminent personalities he'd served in his brilliant career: not only had he been head chef for a sultan and two presidents, but he'd also prepared the last meal for a princess who had died tragically in a car accident. He claimed to be married to an Austrian baroness whose acquaintances included a number of sought-after artists and several sports champions. Clearly, this ship pot-slinger was a total mythomaniac.

I couldn't bear to hear him hold forth for a second longer, so I tore myself loose from his grip.

"I haven't finished," he exhaled, short of breath. "Look at me when I'm talking to you!"

It was the first time that anyone had made such a request and, naturally, complying was out of the question. I pushed the cook away, and my hair slapped him in the process.

My Fatalities, however, reacted in a whole other way: they saw red. Carried away by the fury boiling in their retinas, they opened wide like the jaws of a lion and roared in the cook's face.

Stiff as a post, lips contorted in a hideous grimace, he went over the railing without putting up the least resistance, without trying to grab onto something, without even making a sound. He dropped like lead into the sea and disappeared in the gelatinous mass of medusae with a resounding splat.

Tentacles quickly coiled around his paralyzed head, palpated his chubby face, felt the heat of his exposed jowls, brutally lacerated his skull, shamelessly infiltrated the first orifice they encountered. Flayed by burns, blistered by venom, the cook's face was now nothing more than a soup of incandescent blood, at the centre of which floated the two white globes of his horrified eyes, like two blobs of congealed fat.

A little later, when my guardian returned to the stateroom, he found me sitting dutifully in the armchair, in the same position he'd left me, ready to give him all my attention.

"We'll reach our first port of call day after tomorrow," he announced. "You'll come ashore with me, of course."

I wasn't able to rejoice at this; I was too shaken. By the violence of my Henchwomen. By their rage that I couldn't contain. By the gravity of the crime in which they'd made me complicit.

I barely noticed that I was only half-watching the shipowner. I hadn't emerged unscathed from my experience with the cook. I had acquired a new ocular ability, one I share with the chameleon and a species of fish called the sand lance: focal divergence. Able to move independently, my ocular globes can follow different fixation axes and simultaneously focus on two different objects – which explains my ability to sleep with one eye open.

While one of my Strabismuses remained focussed on the shipowner, the other's gaze flitted about in the stateroom before taking off through the porthole. The sea had become black and unfathomable once again. The ship travelled into the night, marooning in that silent tomb the witness to my Abominations, forever muzzled.

The world that the shipowner had promised to show me was reduced, in practice, to a single object: his own person. As of the first port of call, we acquired the habit of strolling on the streets with him walking in front and me trailing on his heels, my gaze glued to his occiput, since I had to follow his every movement.

Thanks to the divergent power of my sight, I would cheat and keep only one eye on him. With the other, I admired the rooftops and chimneys, the belfries and campaniles, the turrets and obelisks. Every place we entered, I'd be so fascinated by the coffered ceilings, friezes, transept crossings, column capitals, and dome mosaics that I'd forget to look down, almost losing my footing on the stairs. With my Voracities open wide, I'd try to devour it all – the shapes, colours, light, shadows – and blink only at the very last moment. Sound, which had been my guide for so long, had now become mere background noise.

The shipowner was well known in the ports where we dropped anchor. To the people he met, he would present me as his ward. Most of them would examine me with curiosity and, thanks to the glasses, I could watch them on the sly, spy on or even stare at them at leisure without seeming impolite.

I scrutinized the texture of the hair, the pigmentation of the skin, the relief of the nose, the curvature of the lips, the angle of the chin, the volume of the cheek-bones, the pattern of the wrinkles – all the elements that come in countless variations and are put together in infinite permutations. I could never have imagined that humanity could have so many faces.

I was disconcerted by the constant animation of the features, the agitation of the eyebrows, the transformation of the smiles. I would try to decipher the enigma of the expressions but would just end up getting lost in the maze of their fluctuating and ambiguous meanings. The gaze's erratic foraging made me particularly distrustful: in it I detected an attempt to lure as well as conceal.

Previously, I'd only had the opportunity to study eyes in illustrated books. Yet even the most skilled artists haven't been able to reproduce, in all their complexity, the precise shape of the lids, the delicate fringe of the lashes, the flecks of light sparkling on the surface of the cornea, or the jagged stained glass of the iris, with its architectural festoons and rosace of furrows, as clear as water or as tenebrous as the night ...

How could I not envy the normality of these eyes, when I imagined mine to be the most horrible hybrids that nature could produce? Meanwhile, my terrible Infections kept still behind their glasses. But I knew that their calm was superficial and that they were champing at the bit. Like the medusae, they were waiting for their next prey, and it was only a question of time before they would strike again.

As the months went by, my guardian's jealousy became pathological. He would accuse me of neglect at the briefest lapse of attention. He'd set thousands of traps and drag me along to public places to test my concentration. We went to all the ship christenings, dined in crowded restaurants, frequented sports tournaments – and I'd be in serious trouble if I ever gave in to the myriad attempts at distraction.

One time, as we were leaving a stadium, the crowd was so dense and boisterous that we got separated. What better opportunity to give my guardian the slip and escape his clutches, if only for an afternoon? So I let myself drift with this human swell and kept on walking after it had dispersed.

I ended up in a public square, at the centre of which stood a fountain eroded by time. The water flowing into a basin greened by lichen gushed from the hollowed eyes of a Medusa sculpted in stone and from the mouths of the serpents crowning her head.

On ancient pottery, Medusa is always depicted with a grotesque face and converging eyes. Painters and sculptors have made her into a sorrowful figure, with a gaze that's more panic-stricken than petrifying. Yet this fountain's Gorgon had a belligerent brow, a raptor's nose, a predatory mouth; her archaic face seemed to be racked with an uncontrollable rage born in the womb.

Through her eyes, she spat her rage at the fate that had made her a monster and vomited her vengeance on those who dared to look upon her. She was terrifying and yet inspired no terror in me. On the contrary, she seemed familiar, and I smiled at her as I would've smiled at my reflection in the mirror.

The bells of a nearby church reminded me of the hour, and I reluctantly started making my way back. To get to the harbour, I had to move away from the brightly lit boulevards and take the shadowy lanes of the outskirts where crime is so commonplace that nobody notices it. A light drizzle started to fall, and I was soon accosted by some guy smoking under a café awning.

With a big bushy head screwed onto a pipsqueak body, he looked like a cup-and-ball toy. His stern physiognomy was not welcoming; he also had caterpillar eyebrows, a nicotinish complexion, and nails half mooned by grime. He was wearing a ribbed sweater in a sinister grey and a scarf artistically tied around his neck. His name was Fleischer, and he happened to be a painter.

"I'm surprised you've never heard of me," he said. "If you want to get out of the rain, my studio's just around the corner."

I had no intention of accepting his invitation, but my Deplorabilities smelled adventure. They were riveted on the painter and made me follow him down a back lane to an attic located above a dilapidated dyeworks, whose fumes made the air, already sticky with tobacco, even more noxious. The wind blew in through the broken squares of the sole window and rain leaked through the roof.

"Don't touch anything," he said, lighting the wick of a sputtering lamp and a new cigarette with the same match.

Was he afraid that I'd mess up the clutter, which was covered in more soot than a burned-down place? Ashtrays overflowed with mounds of chewed cigarette butts, mould flourished at the bottom of soiled cups, a rolled-up pile of dirty rags languished in a corner.

Fleischer's paintings were scattered all around the walls. There were at least a hundred small frames, all depicting the same subject: the artist himself. These self-portraits, painted in hues of asphalt, tar, charcoal, and creosote, had been violently executed and chiselled by murderous cross-hatching that had torn the canvas in places. Some had been splattered with coffee, others burned with cigarettes. Paintbrushes with torn bristles, graphite sticks, and spilled bottles of India ink lay strewn around the floor like weapons at a crime scene.

Fiddling with his cigarette with a haughty air that didn't hide his bitterness, his envy, or his spite, Fleischer admitted that no gallery was interested in exhibiting his work and that he hadn't managed to sell a single painting in his entire life. Then, with no other preamble, he swooped down on me and ripped off my glasses.

"I thought you could be my muse," he said with an embarrassed little laugh, which he quickly suppressed by clearing his throat. "I'll paint your portrait. Come on, open your eyes!"

I felt besieged by this summary invasion and summons to surrender. I thought of nothing but how I could retrieve my glasses. Yet my Licentiousnesses were ready to undress – though without rushing things. Their exhibitionism in front of the cook had been too brief and had left them unsatisfied. They now intended to prolong their pleasure.

Beginning a dance of the seven veils, they shed their lashes bit by bit, revealing their seductive lids and various parts of their anatomy, until they had exposed the most intimate folds of their monstrosity. Spread wide in all their outrageousness, they speared their captive prey with their most ardent gaze.

The incredulity on the painter's face gave way to a gasp of astonishment. Horror spread to his eyes and, beneath the caterpillar eyebrows, his pupils caught fire and consumed the irises. Black smoke spread to the corneas, turning even the moribund lids to ash.

I was relieved to feel Fleischer's last breath on my cheek and see the spark die out in his eyes. I left him right where he fell in the middle of his paintings. With his grey complexion and his two pieces of coal, he had become the spitting image of his self-portraits.

Despite being appalled at this new crime, I had to admit that my Wrathfulnesses, which had defended me with such courage, were perhaps, after all, a blessing and a guarantee of my safety.

It goes without saying that this little escapade sounded the death knell for my permission on land. My guardian had been so afraid that he'd lost me, he put me under house arrest, strapped to the armchair, for the rest of the journey. He suspected that I'd been unfaithful to him and his jealousy made him irascible: his mood swings would be followed by periods of sulking that corrupted the air in the entire stateroom.

The months at sea dragged endlessly on, and I would've died of boredom if I'd had to watch him day and night, as he now demanded. Fortunately, my Dishonourabilities had acquired a hypnotic power since the painter's death. With a bit of concentration, I could sink the shipowner into a lethargic sleep and free myself of his perpetual presence for several hours.

I bided my time. In any case, our voyage was coming to an end: a year had already passed since we'd gone to sea, the cargo ship would soon need to be restocked ...

I couldn't help noticing how much my guardian had aged since our departure. He'd lost his hair and his skull was liver-spotted. His hands, their joints swollen with nodules, were wormy with blue veins. His features were wracked by wrinkles, there were dark circles under his eyes, and his eyelids were withered like foreskin.

In truth, my Succubae were slowly sucking the life out of my guardian.

The cargo ship reached the capital's harbour in the dead of winter. The rays of the setting sun crystallized in the icy air before they could provide any warmth.

Despite the severity of the cold, the city – both the upper and lower town – was giddy with the hectic rhythm of Carnival. Lit up by torches, the streets were inundated with horse-drawn carriages and hordes of revellers in advanced states of inebriation, bundled in their wildcat-fur coats, roaring with laughter and singing drinking songs. Their red faces were as grotesque as masks and frightened the horses who were pawing the ground, clouds of steam escaping their nostrils.

My guardian kept glancing behind him with a worried look on his face.

"The benefactors will not give you up so easily and they'll surely try to reclaim you now that you're back in the city," he said. "But don't worry! I won't let them take you. I'll even adopt you if I have to!"

His house was perched on the tip of the promontory, overlooking the city and seaway; the slightest breeze made the rafters creak. The drawing room was inhospitable, all drafty and full of sharp angles. The walls displayed, in niches and under a weak light, models of sailboats, ships in bottles, and sundry objects found in shipwrecked galleys and galleons: a ship's bell covered in barnacles, a bosun's whistle corroded by salt, coins covered in verdigris, a bronze statuette, sabres, nautical instruments ...

I was able to better examine these treasures once the shipowner fell asleep at last in his chair, in particular three medusae reproduced in blown and spun glass, like ones found in natural history museums. Hand-painted in a faded pink, these creatures were so delicate that I didn't dare touch them for fear of breaking them.

The curtains fluttered like ghostly spectres. Looking out at the seaway beyond the oriel window, I felt as though I was floating on a ghost ship from which I wouldn't disembark for an eternity ...

I sensed a slight variation in the density of the shadows outside: a man's silhouette, menacing in its perfect stillness. So the house was being watched, and the benefactors would soon be apprised of my return ...

Just let them try to abduct me if they so wished. Then I'd show them the true mettle of my Furies.

My Ignobilities could not endure being shut up in such a tomb any longer. The night of Mardi Gras, they swelled their crystalline lenses and stalked my guardian's eyelids until he fell asleep sucking his thumb.

I left him in this comatose state, from which he wouldn't emerge until the following day. I was in such a hurry to get out that I didn't even take the time to comb my hair; I grabbed a coat and headed to the old town. The full moon shone through the clouds. The crystals of a fine and densely falling snow were swept up by the wind, seeped down my collar, and stung the skin on my neck; they stuck in my hair, making it look like spiky tentacles.

I didn't bother turning around to check if I was being followed: I was sure that I was and that the benefactors' villain was cunning enough to stay off my radar. Still, I amused myself trying to confuse him by taking the busiest streets possible.

The château was hosting a masquerade ball, and a gang of partiers thronged the entrance, shaking to the blaring music pouring out onto the street. Under a shower of confetti and streamers, they flaunted their faces of sinister sparrows, pearl-studded moons, clowns with jingle bells, and birds with iridescent feathers …

I joined their grotesque pantomime, strangely soothed by the marmoreal stillness of the masks, and found myself nose to nose with an emerald, papier-mâché face of Medusa, crowned with a swarm of sequinned serpents. By the Carnival's subversive inversion, my monstrous nature was being celebrated in all its splendour – with one exception: with her enucleated sockets, this Medusa was disarmed, neutralized, rendered powerless.

Besides, the slits in the mask revealed inoffensive, dull orbs. How could a normal creature understand the weight of an accursed defect, the loneliness of ostracism, the shame of being an abomination against nature? What did this pitiful impostor know about the predatory hunger that racked my pupils even at that very moment? What would she do if I unmasked my Grotesqueries? Would she start screaming or keel over?

I escaped the masquerade ball and drifted to the terrace where ice sculptures extolled the heroes of our history: explorers and founders perched on pedestals, trappers and missionaries in canoes, patriots and generals brandishing flags, athletes and strongmen lit up by torches ...

The bell in the cathedral rang the twelve strokes of midnight, announcing the end of Carnival and the beginning of Lent. Sobering up all of a sudden, the curious onlookers started dispersing, leaving a few recalcitrant revellers behind. I didn't see my pursuer among them and feared that I might've lost him for good. I was so set on confronting him, however, that I gave him one more chance and waited for him in the empty pavilion.

Yet to my great disappointment, an entirely different

person turned up on the threshold: some upstart university student. His fleshy face was partly hidden by a cardboard domino mask that stood lopsided on the bridge of his bulbous nose and made him look even more drunk. He was covered in snow from head to foot and his sparse curls, twisted by the wind, formed two frozen horns on top of his head.

"Do you have a suitor?" he asked me with a fake accent.

"I'm not looking for one."

"But sometimes, love finds us ..."

He told me about his miserable evening, which had started well enough: he'd managed to crash the masquerade ball at the château, though he hadn't been invited – an offence with which this boozer obviously had much experience. Having partaken of the libations a bit too excessively, his disgraceful behaviour had drawn the attention of the personnel. He'd been unmasked and unceremoniously thrown into a snowbank. The humiliation hadn't affected his presumptuousness.

"I've decided to court you," he announced, "and I cherish the prospect of taking you someplace more intimate. Come on, Carnival is over: take off your mask and show me your pretty eyes!"

This time, I didn't wait for my Cataclysms to go on the offensive. With the impetuousness of a timid person, I removed my glasses as though rising to a challenge and shot the student my most glacial look.

He had a cast of the eye, if not a slight squint, that got worse the instant he saw me. His eyelids started to tremble, making his ice-covered lashes tinkle like aeolian harps. He tried to turn away, but my hair twisted around the buttons of his jacket and held him in place. He was caught in my snare, and I froze him on the spot.

His cold sweat crystallized, coating his skin like frost. His nose went white with chilblain. A dribble of winey mucus, escaped from his atrophied lips, froze on his badly shaven chin. His eyes rolled upwards with the effort to evade the sight of my Harpies. Too late: they had forever turned to ice.

When I left the pavilion, the student was already stone cold. No one would ever be able to distinguish him from the ice statutes of this glorious park.

As for my Detestables, I blushed thinking of their delinquency and the depravity with which I had just disclosed them. Their indecency filled me with disgust. As you can see, shame hadn't yet let go of me.

My Ogressions had stuffed themselves with the last specks of life in the student's eyes – a welcome diversion, of course – yet they weren't quite sated. They still hoped to confront my pursuer and so made me wander all over the city until dawn. I felt his presence behind me, but he kept his distance and synchronized his steps to mine so perfectly that he remained invisible. He was toying with me, testing my patience. At last, I had a worthy adversary.

Walking back to the shipowner's house, I passed some people who had put away their tawdry rags, donned austere threads, and swapped their colourful masks for gaunt faces. Whispering gravely, they headed to the Ash Wednesday service, their heels dragging the ball and chain of contrition behind them.

A child's laugh suddenly shattered this funereal silence – a rippling, insolent laugh. In a courtyard, a boy had trapped his sister and was going out of his way to pelt her with snowballs. The little girl had lost her mittens and kept blowing on her hands to warm them. Having nothing but her back for a shield, she called a truce, but her brother bombarded her with even more gusto.

What fun could the boy be getting out of this brutal and belligerent game? Did he, just like the benefactors, have such an evil mind that he'd abuse those weaker than him, or was he unaware of the effects of his strength? It's true that most boys don't seem to feel pain when they push, fight, and shove each other, laughing; the fear of getting hurt doesn't hold them back. Maybe they, like me, have the ability to anaesthetize pain, which would explain their constant advantage. Suffering must seem insignificant when one seeks only victory ...

My indignant Lamiae craved to intervene on behalf of the little girl and if I hadn't quickly walked away, they would've been capable of scaring the poor boy. To calm myself, I went into a chapel where the Ash Wednesday service had just ended. Some of the faithful lingered in their pews, heads prostrate. I sat down out of the way in the last row and looked at my surroundings with curiosity, since this was my first time in a church.

The only light came from a fifteen-arm, pyramidal candelabrum that stood on the altar, the candles of which were almost burned out. The silence encouraged repentance and atonement. So I had the opportunity to examine my crimes.

I had tried to convince myself that my Striges were the only ones guilty of these murders, while I was just an eyewitness. In truth, I, too, bore the burden of responsibility because I hadn't stopped them. Yet if I really examined my conscience, I couldn't feel any remorse or compassion for my victims. I even took great delight in remembering their deaths.

I had to admit to myself then that I'd lost my last shreds of humanity. I truly was a monster.

A short little man reeking of Florida Water appeared beside me. His elongated head, bloated belly, and tiny feet made him look like one of those roly-poly toys whose round bottom is weighted so that it always rights itself when pushed over.

He squeezed me to the back of the pew, which bent under his weight. He sat like some vaudeville impresario, thighs spread open, ankles crossed, feet resting on the kneeler. Leering at me, he tidied his hair, which had been waved with a curling iron and dyed with laundry bluing, and straightened up the periwinkle on his lapel. He took the opportunity to run his hand along my flank and, feigning clumsiness, apologized with such insincerity that it was embarrassing.

The man, whose name was Bleury, was a town historian and awaited only an imperceptible sign of encouragement to start griping about the chapel. He pointed out the walls, full of votive marble plaques in memory of children who had died. Their age at time of death and the cause of their demise were inscribed under their name.

I may be a monster, but I was not insensitive to the fate of these children. I was upset to learn that some had been struck by illness and that many had had accidents while innocently playing: they'd set themselves on fire while messing with matches, they'd fallen out a window, they'd been crushed under a horse's hooves, buried under a snow fort and torn to pieces by a snowblower, run over by a truck while riding a bicycle, electrocuted by a kite, scalded by jams, poisoned by medicine, swept away by a flooding river, or, like Suzanne, they'd drowned in a lake's treacherous waters …

"I don't really like children," Monsieur Bleury said, wiping a tear from his eye with a handkerchief embroidered with his initials. "However, I really appreciate young girls."

On the altar, a single candle still burned. Taking advantage of the dim light, the historian leaned over and whispered in my ear:

"I want to show you something."

I thought that he was going to draw my attention to some vestige of the chapel's foundation or an episode in its history. Instead, he unbuttoned his coat and held it open. In an effort to hide his roundness, he wore his pants cinched above the belly button, so that his fly, stretched to the max, looked like it was about to tear.

He cracked his joints before unbuckling his belt: the buttons above the zipper popped off, the fly ripped open, and he proudly took out his prick by pulling on the foreskin.

I held back my rage so as not to alarm him and even gave him a smile.

"What a coincidence! I too have something to show you."

Just before the last candle could burn out, I lowered my glasses to the tip of my nose and let him see my

Ghouls. Flabbergasted, he let out a strangled gasp and stopped breathing instantly. Deprived of oxygen, his skin quickly turned cyanotic, as though bluish methylene flowed in his veins. His lips took on a cobalt tint, the bags under his eyes looked like purplish bruises, his extremities turned navy blue, and his balls indigo.

I left the historian in this disgraceful state and quietly exited the chapel, imagining the scandal that would erupt when his body was found. I have no doubt that he'll go down in our city's sordid history. They might even put up a votive plaque for him in the chapel.

I returned exhausted from my night of wandering. I'd hoped to have some time to rest my Appalingnesses before the shipowner woke up, but he was waiting for me in the drawing room. While I was gone, he'd emerged from his torpor and, bewildered by my absence, looked for me all over the house. Left on his own, deprived of the constant attention he'd grown accustomed to and to which he was now addicted, he'd collapsed on the drawing-room carpet, writhing in the throes of withdrawal.

"Where have you been?" he asked, shivering.

In the hearth, the fire was almost out. I poked the embers, put a log in the andirons, and watched it catch fire before answering.

"I went to the masquerade ball at the château and saw some ice sculptures."

"You could've run into one of the benefactors, you reckless creature. What were you thinking?"

I shrugged my shoulders before going to sit in my usual spot in front of him. He was feverish and at the end of his rope.

"I know how to defend myself. I met two importunate assailants, and all I had to do was show them my eyes to cool off their ardour."

Despite his weakness, he found the energy to be wracked with jealousy.

"You're my pupil! You've no right to look at another beside me. You've betrayed me!"

I didn't like his tone, inquisitional and insinuating all at once, so I said rather abruptly, "I was unfaithful to you, in fact. And it wasn't the first time."

He was at my mercy, and I wasn't feeling merciful. I wanted to play with him a bit, torment his heart, strike fear into his eyes. So I told him how I'd congealed the eyes of the fondling cook, carbonized those of the disrobing painter, crystallized those of the lecherous student, and cyanotized those of the exhibitionist historian. I described the terror of my victims and the atrociousness of their deaths. I didn't spare him any details of my murders and even confessed to that of my father. But in the shipowner's twisted lips, I saw nothing but incredulity and an inability to see that the hour of retribution had come.

"You ungrateful girl!" he moaned through clenched teeth. "Your eyes belong to me. Give them back!"

It was the first time that I was going to remove my glasses in front of the shipowner and, despite the familiarity induced by a year of promiscuity on the cargo ship, I felt more embarrassed than in front of a stranger. I didn't give in to the impulse of my modesty, however, but opened my lids wide like carriage doors and, with my most obscene countenance, stunned my guardian.

With an albatross's cry, he clenched his jaw. The tendons of his neck went taut like the tightrope of a funambulist. His head shot backwards, his neck cracked, his spine braced itself. Showing him no mercy, I shrivelled his corneas and sclerosed his scleras, crystallized his crystalline lenses and calcified the capillaries of his retinas, irradiated his irises to a lacklustre blue. I continued to torment him long after he'd expired.

My deceased guardian, once so well put together, was now nothing more than a wreck. I had sufficiently watched over his living body not to feel obliged to watch over his remains. So I left him, without even bothering to close his eyes.

Before departing, I took one last look around, making sure I hadn't forgotten anything. I noticed that in the niches of the drawing room, the small glass medusae had vanished.

Outside, it had grown milder, but a snowstorm engulfed the city like flakes of ash after a fire. Struggling against the squalls with my head down, I walked towards the last place where I could've found refuge.

I followed the main boulevard until I recognized the red-brick façade of my paternal home. Trudging up the stairs, I noticed that the steps were broken, the banister rusted, the window frames rotted, and, for some reason, this state of dilapidation gave me a kick.

The door knocker, long neglected, was encrusted with verdigris. The oxidation had seeped into all the details of the serpentine head, but curiously had spared Medusa's eyes, which shone in the storm as though the brass had just been polished. I knocked a few times before the creaking door opened at last on the sad figure of my mother in a frayed peignoir, her hair loose, her skin sallow. She was only a faded version of her former beauty but hadn't lost any of her bite.

"As soon as I heard that you'd run away from the institute, I knew you'd show up here someday," she said, cinching the belt of her peignoir. "If you hope to squeeze some money out of me, you're too late. Your sisters have already taken everything valuable from me."

I assured her that all I wanted was a room for the night. She took her time assessing the gravity of the bad weather before letting me come in – on one condition: "You must leave once the storm is over."

I followed her into the living room, while she continued to whine about my older sisters, now married, who never sent her news or came to visit.

"What evil twist of fate has sent you to me in their place?"

She didn't ask me to sit down, so I remained standing. I looked in vain for the family carpets on the bare parquet. On the walls, dark outlines indicated the absence of paintings, the mantle over the fireplace was devoid of ornaments, and the echoing emptiness made my mother's voice sound even more cavernous.

"I've always feared the day when you'd come back to haunt me. You wear glasses now, but you can't fool me: I know what hides behind them, I know what you are. You are Evil, Medusa! Original sin personified! I knew it the instant when, in your crib, you opened your eyes for the first time. How could such an abomination have come from my womb?"

The disgust stamped in her eyes was all too familiar to me: I'd seen it every time she'd arranged my hair over my brow, every time she'd pushed me away from her skirts. My presence was a daily reminder of the blood tie between her and an aberration, a crime against nature, an impurity. She had preferred to disown me rather than be judged, sullied by my disgrace, and banished from society.

There she stood, the origin of the shame I felt for my Aversions: in what she'd passed down to me by teaching me to hate them, to hide them, to fear mirrors, and to live apart from the rest of humanity.

"I thought our family was saved the day your father found an institute that would take you at last," she insisted on adding. "His untimely death put an end to all my hopes."

"If it's any consolation," I said with vindictiveness, "he didn't die alone. I was with him, and my eyes were the last thing he saw."

In response, my mother let out an interminable wail. The outrage deformed her facial features, rage blew out of her nostrils, bile turned her skin a bluish green, and when she started pulling her hair, I swear to you that her resemblance to the Medusa of the doorknocker was unmistakable.

I retreated to the stairs and, trembling, hurried up to my room. I'm really at a loss to tell you why my mother frightened me so much. We are always someone else's monster, I suppose. One thing is certain, she was still mine.

What would've happened if my parents, out of charity, had kept me at home instead of sending me to the institute? I would've willingly remained shut away in my room, I wouldn't have asked for anything, I would've made them forget I existed ... I wouldn't have had to defend myself against strangers.

However, would the comfort of home, in the absence of family affection, have been enough to preserve my innocence? Would my human side have dominated the natural inclinations of my Hydras, or would they have ultimately emerged to express their violence and impose the same burdensome fate on me?

Such were the thoughts that assailed me when I saw my childhood bedroom again. From my adult height, the room seemed to be squeezed in by the walls and squashed down by the ceiling. What's more, it had been transformed into a sitting room. There was no trace of my bed, my dresser, or the small objects that I'd left behind: the memory of my existence had been obliterated from the place.

I went up to the window that gives onto the main boulevard. Outside, the sky and ground were still invisible, and I had to pierce the quilted whiteness of the snow before I could make out the figure nonchalantly leaning against the streetlight, hands stuffed in the pockets of a coat with the collar raised up. I thought that my pursuer's perseverance was admirable – heroic even. I was almost flattered to be the object of such determination. The benefactors had, after all, chosen their henchman well. But it mattered little to me: one look, and his fate would be sealed.

I would've liked to dismiss him from my mind the way you discard a worthless card in a card game. My Concupiscences, however, could not tear themselves away and scrutinized him with shameless voyeurism: they admired the determination of the shoulders, the solidity of the pelvis, the robustness of the thighs, the virility of the posture ...

Intoxicated by their scopic excitation, they started pulsating, emitting a suction sound that had nothing human about it. On my cheeks, not tears but a milky, viscous liquid with a raw odour and seminal taste soon began to trickle, its unknown source refusing to run dry. From my sockets, I was squirting fluid like that fountain of Medusa's head that I had so admired ...

Out of all the manifestations of my Empusas, I must admit that this libidinal discharge inspired the greatest shame in me. With my sight blurred, I quickly turned away from the window and ran to wash myself.

The cat-and-mouse game into which I'd been dragged against my will had gone on too long. The time had come to finish with the benefactors' villain – and I knew exactly where to lure him to deliver the coup de grâce.

When I left my mother's house (without saying good-bye, needless to say), the storm had abated and the main streets had been plowed, but the sidewalks were still carpeted with snow, which muffled my footsteps. To make it easier for my pursuer, I made sure to leave clear footprints behind me and headed towards the bridge, until at last I saw the crenellated turrets of the aquarium.

The snow had discouraged visitors, which aided my plan. I strolled through empty galleries under the indifferent gaze of indolent fish, sinister specimens of the aquatic fauna of our majestic seaway, as well as our lakes and rivers, looking lost out of their element. In water made murky by sediment, trout and brown bullheads built castles in the air; the golden scales of bass looked dulled; the eels and pike stayed camouflaged in the algae; the pumpkinseeds and plaice hid in the sand. My victim was on my heels; he was hooked, all I had to do was drag him into my net.

I left behind this torpid murkiness and stepped into the medusa gallery – the place from where my two sisters had derived my nickname. The luminous undulations emanating from the aquariums filled the darkened gallery with the iridescent green of a sea cave. All around me, the medusae advanced along vertical axes, spitting water from their mouths either upward or downward.

As I approached, they drew closer, writhing against the glass panes. At last, I could examine these fragile creatures up close and marvel at their strange anatomy, their unreal translucence and graceful means of propulsion. Like burlesque seductresses, they pulled their petticoats above their sylph legs and slender thighs, shamelessly exposing their red-glowing gonads. In the aquarium mirror, each was a reflection of me.

An intrusive shadow descended like the night, darkening this luminous spectacle. I smelled tobacco and felt the incandescence of breath on my nape. The time of the duel had come. With determination, I took off my glasses and turned around at once. Why would I have hesitated? I thought I was invincible.

I won't pretend to offer an accurate account of our first face-to-face encounter. After all, I only know my own perspective – which is a reflection of yours, as though in a mirror. You must admit, however, that we were both marked by a fate of mythological proportions. For if I was Medusa, you could only be Perseus, come to kill me.

You had the physique, if not the beauty, of a hero: virility exuded from all your pores. There was something intensely visceral about your chiselled cheekbones, something primal about your gangster scar, something carnal about the lips emerging from your black beard.

You were cast in a different mould than my previous victims, and I didn't make the mistake of underestimating you. Into your confident eyes, I plunged my Swords of Damocles up to the hilt, and even twisted them better to ravage you.

You took the blow and held my gaze unblinkingly, showing no weakness whatsoever. Your resistance threw me off balance: I couldn't understand why you hadn't turned to stone. I redoubled my efforts but was repelled by the bronze shield of your eyes.

Not only were you not afraid of my Grim Reapers, but they didn't even seem to put you off. You examined them with fascination, as though trying to memorize their particularities, narrowing your eyes to capture certain details, tilting your head to appreciate them from another angle.

You were devouring me with your eyes, and I felt more naked than if I had no clothes on – because it was one thing to undress before a dying victim and quite another to suffer the sustained attention of a formidable adversary.

The glimmers of the aquariums reflected in the crystal of your irises, silvering them like mirrors in which I risked seeing myself if I kept looking at you for much longer. I was still terrified of discovering my true likeness. The shame of my Obscenities rose up in me with the impetuous surge of an eruption and my lashes started to flutter, feeling faint. Before being petrified by my own reflection, I retreated and hurried to put my glasses back on.

I asked you if you were going to cut off my head, like in mythology, and you burst out laughing – with a laughter come from time immemorial, amplified by your cavernous thorax, which made your teeth gleam through the bristles of your beard.

"I'm just a modest abductor, paid to bring you back to the institute, by whatever force necessary, before the new moon."

"Not all that modest. How can you stand the sight of my Execrations?"

You answered as if it was obvious, "You have the eyes of a woman, Medusa. You shouldn't be ashamed."

Can one simple look open our eyes? The one you gave me shook up all my certainty.

I had not foreseen the possibility that my Plagues of

Egypt could be anything but revolting, nor that they could be the prerogative of femininity. Shame had so steadily held me in its yoke that I had always sided with others' impressions of me, accepted their judgment, and assimilated their version without questioning their validity. I had endured the blood rushing to my face, the lead weight crushing my lungs, the painful piercing of my heart that came with every humiliation. Alienated from my nature, I had offended it by hiding it behind hair, blindfolds, glasses.

Since my childhood, shame had served as my conscience. It had controlled my life, dictated my choices, presided over my decisions. The constriction of my liberum arbitrium, the pulverization of my amour-propre, the virulent hatred of my own being had not only unsighted, enucleated, blinded me; it had also clipped my wings, bound my hands, sawed off my legs. Shame petrified me, because I was saturated with it. It was an adversary more debilitating than my Adversities, and the time had come to free myself from its tyranny.

"The new moon is in thirteen days," you said. "The benefactors can wait."

Without putting up any resistance, I offered you my arm and let myself be ravished.

I was not surprised that you'd take me to the roughest neighbourhood in the city, down some forgotten lane by the ramparts: where else would you have lived?

I hesitated on the threshold of your lair, put off by your shack of sooty planks and windows plastered with newspaper. Then the door opened, and the shimmer of an enchanting casket blinded me. Silver, ebony, crystal, mother-of-pearl, amber, coral, enamel, and cameo: in front of all these precious materials, I no longer knew where to turn my gaze.

There was no question in my mind that the provenance of the precious metalwork, art objects, and paintings was dubious. But when I recognized, among these ill-gotten wares, the small glass medusae of the shipowner, I truly knew whom I was dealing with.

You must be exceptionally skilled to have committed forty-eight robberies in private homes while eluding the sleuths of our police force. Your crimes didn't weigh on your conscience: you stored your spoils here before fencing them to receivers. Without pride or shame, as though your profession was banal and respectable, you hid none of your offences from me. On this subject, at least, you were an open book.

Despite the detached tone with which you recounted your adventures, I imagine that you must've felt some humiliation when you were finally caught red-handed, last year, while trying to steal two miserable silver goblets ... You must've also been shaken when the judge sentenced you to four years in prison.

These are feelings I can understand, believe me. After all, I've gone before the same judge, in the private wing of the institute, and I'm familiar with his intransigence. So I can't blame you for making a secret deal with this benefactor-devil: for his leniency, you'd agreed to abduct me.

For months, you'd kept watch at the harbour, waiting for our cargo ship to return, and as soon as it arrived, you'd followed me. You'd seen the state in which I'd left my victims. So you hadn't been unaware of the danger I posed when you'd faced me in the medusa gallery. You must've been very sure of yourself to confront me like that ...

No more than I, you couldn't go against your nature, either: you had the soul of a thief, and I represented just another share of your plunder. I saw it in your covetous eyes when you said, "You can take off your glasses now."

I don't think you can appreciate the difficulty that the simple gesture of taking off a pair of glasses represented for me. How could you? Shame doesn't hamper you in the least: you think of it as something imposed, false, even fraudulent. You hide nothing, you don't justify your methods, you don't look for excuses, you defy decorum, you mock mockery, you are impervious to insults. Have you felt shame even once in your life?

Yet I'm grateful to you for giving me a few hours to get used to my nudity. The ambient air irritated my ocular globes, and I first had to master the protective reflex of drawing them back into their shell. Whenever my lids would lower, I'd raise them valiantly, even though I had the impression, in the harsh daylight, that I was insulting decency and serving up my obscenity to you.

Clumsy, like a fledgling just learning to fly, I didn't venture too far: I started by exploring my immediate environment, then timidly expanded my field of vision. I groped my way over the many objects of your loot, striving to keep my balance by clinging to the relief of the candelabra, coffers, and urns.

At last, dusk reached the windows of your lair, subduing my immodesty in indulgent shadows – and I launched into the unknown. I was emboldened to observe you surreptitiously while you read the headlines in our local paper about the mysterious deaths of two individuals at Carnival. Instead of listening to you, I watched your gestures and facial expressions closely, wondering if I'd ever possess your enviable ease without my glasses.

With a weary sigh, you stopped reading and dropped the newspaper on the floor. Your eyes – those unscrupulous rogues, always ready to take what didn't belong to you, and of which your sticky fingers were but mere extensions – undressed mine with an impetuous gaze. You came and stood before me, taking my head in your hands, our faces so close our lashes could've crossed swords.

I didn't have time to fight off the attack. With the dexterity of a conjurer, you mugged my lashes, robbed my lids, raided my lacrimal caruncles. You deflowered the hymen of my crystalline lenses and entered me by small infractions, engorging every filament of my irises, spreading their carnal quivers through the tributaries of my capillaries.

My pupils throbbed in synch with yours, following along with the sustained drumming of your pulsations, getting intoxicated by their increasing ardour. In a fit of boundless voracity, I dilated them even more and offered my retinas to your pillage, letting you despoil me completely: after all, you weren't ripping anything from me that I didn't want to be rid of.

Just as I was about to surrender my last entrenchment to you, my Bestialities started exuding their milky fluid, and you groaned with contentment as you licked it. Your moist lips whispered in my ear, "You are a force of nature, Medusa."

Afraid that my climax would unleash latent and unsuspected vices, I shut my lids with a snap of bewilderment and dismay. I had just discovered that, through a perverse causal link, the source of shame is also that of the greatest voluptuous pleasure.

After a week during which we barely closed our eyes, I had discarded any last inkling of modesty. Released from my dark glass barriers, my brow cleared of all obstruction, I had returned to a natural state – the one in which I'd come into the world. I had rediscovered the innocence before the fall and now lived in the blessed ignorance of my nakedness.

Eager to make up for the time I'd wasted hiding behind a mask, I walked around your lair unabashedly, lids wide open, corneas exposed to the air. You'd watch me on the sly, but I'd pretend not to notice and keep exploring.

My gaze would land on whatever attracted it and, with a naive lasciviousness, caress the materials, palpate the rough surfaces, probe the crevices. Little by little, the wounds of my past humiliations began to cauterize, and the painful feeling of inferiority that had kept me prostrate lessened.

I liked feeling your eyes on mine. I amused myself seducing you with my lashes while you winked at me. As soon as our lashes embraced, our gazes would penetrate each other and remain welded together, caught in a continuous loop. We were linked by their chain of invisible fervour, fused in their perpetual tape, powerless to interrupt their coupling. The same intent fuelled our pupils, the same trance enthralled them. I never wanted to leave your eyes ...

But at the last moment, shame would cut short my orgasm by occluding my Carnalities. You'd then have to lavish your most convincing compliments on me to get me to open them again.

Don't think for a second that I doubted your sincerity when you professed your admiration and desire. They say that beauty is in the eye of the beholder, and perhaps you have the ability to see through imperfections, to see beyond appearances ... Though I rather suspect that you have a fascination for ugliness, a penchant for the morbid, a perverse attraction to the grotesque.

Either way, it seemed clear to me that you were blinded by a fleeting passion and that the scales would eventually fall from your eyes.

"You should be more careful," I told you. "You could be struck down at any moment."

With a disapproving shake of your head, you retorted, "Look, Medusa, you know very well that your eyes aren't dangerous."

"As a matter of fact, I don't know it. I've never seen them in my life."

You were so stunned that I was afraid I'd turned you to stone. Then I committed the fatal error of admitting the terror that mirrors inspired in me.

Your face remained impassive: only the corners of your lips lifted slightly and a vulpine smile cracked your coal-black beard. You'd just uncovered the secret of my vulnerability.

The waning moon had tapered to its last crescent when we left your lair. I put on my glasses out of reflex, but I could've done without them: the streets were so deserted we passed no one, not even a cat. The weather was dreadful; the wind blew between the ice-covered façades and drove at our backs. I didn't know where you were taking me, because you wanted to surprise me.

We crossed the river and stopped in front of the exhibition grounds, which were closed for the season. In the blink of an eye, you picked the lock of the main gate, and we sneaked onto the grounds, guided by the flashlight with which you'd come supplied – the flash-light of a true thief with a narrow beam and whose heavy handle, you told me with a wink, could also be used to break heads.

The site resembled a vast necropolis where the palace of industry, racetrack, agricultural buildings, grandstand, and amphitheatre served as monumental sepulchres. In the amusement park, behind the skeletal frames of rollercoasters, stood a carnival stand painted black: the house of mirrors.

There was no way I was going to enter this death trap, so I grumbled and complained. But you made me understand that I could no longer turn back: to free myself of shame, I had to pass this trial by fire (or rather, in this case, by mirror) and see myself with my own eyes at last. For nothing to contaminate my point of view, I had to confront what I dreaded most, alone.

"You have nothing to fear. Trust me."

Despite my apprehensions, I gave in as though I was resigning to the inevitable. Besides, hadn't I always known that this moment of truth would come sooner or later?

When you handed me the flashlight, I reminded you that my night vision was excellent, but you insisted, closing the door behind me:

"Mirrors need light to reflect."

The place smelled of mildew, the floorboards sagged under the least transfer of weight from one foot to the other. The flashlight beam bounced off the polished mirrors, revealing their spiderweb cracks, rippled surfaces, black spots, and all the greasy fingerprints left on them.

I'd always been skilled at avoiding reflective surfaces, but it was impossible to do that here. My formidable stature and head bristling with viperine hair would've been more than enough to make an impression on me. Yet at every turn, I could also see my silhouette from a different angle, distorted by concave, convex, or rippled mirrors, which transformed me into a Lilliputian with a gigantic head and muscular thighs, a harpy with an elongated neck and raging hair, a grotesque contortionist with ophidian movements ... so many terrible figures that would've struck fear into anyone in a house of horrors and which I approached timidly, since, I swear to you, their hostility seemed to be threatening me personally. Had you sent me here to remind me of my monstrosity?

The route of the maze seemed simple enough, yet the reflective echoes of the landmarks turned it into a mystifying labyrinth. Deprived of my sense of orientation, I ended up in the central room somewhat inadvertently. The mirrors here were smooth, but they formed a kaleidoscope with myriad facets, in which I was multiplied into an infinite, dizzying horde that disoriented me.

The idea that I'd formed of my face had always remained vague, like cotton-wool fog with amorphous holes instead of orifices. I didn't recognize myself in this stranger's face, which, on the contrary, had angular features, a defined bone structure, an imperious nose, a sharp mouth, a determined chin. Impossible to read any emotion in it: no expression animated me, no frown betrayed my dark mood, no tension suggested my inner struggle.

My face, of a uniform pallor, seemed to be carved out of marble, and the glasses' lenses cut two black circles into it, like empty sockets in the middle of a skull. I tried to smile but only managed to curl up my lips, revealing clenched teeth. I must confess to you that I would've preferred to face the abominable grimaces of the Furies and Graeae rather than this inscrutable, dead head.

How did my Murderesses cause death? I didn't know what shocking colour, what corrupt form nature had given them – in any case, it would've been impossible for me to imagine. But I had no doubt that they were lethally atrocious. Behind the glasses, I sensed their fatal malice, their unbridled force, their appetite for destruction ...

A premonition of imminent danger assailed me. My jaw clenched, my breath stopped short, and my nerves stretched taut like the tightrope of a funambulist ... Before I could be petrified on the spot, I threw the flashlight at the mirrors. With a clatter of broken glass, the prismatic room shattered into a thousand splinters, the grotesque horde disbanded, and my reflection was pulverized at last.

I wanted to break all the mirrors in the world. To tell you the truth, I wasn't ready to look into the deformities of my heart or contemplate my soul in all its ugliness.

Were you surprised to see me come out of the maze alive? Saddened that I'd failed your test? Disappointed that I'd proved to be so faint-hearted? Relieved that you still had the advantage over me? That's certain, since when you saw me come out without my glasses on, hair constellated with shards of mirrors, you turned to me with derision, "You pretend to be a monster, but you're afraid of your own reflection."

Frankly, you could've shown me some compassion: you could see very well that my failure had broken me. Besides, how could you have had the gall to minimize the devastating power of my Horsewomen of the Apocalypse? As far as I know, my victims had not departed this life in an ecstatic state. I had myself endured their ascendency and narrowly escaped their deathly grip …

Though I had reason enough to fear them and trembled at the thought of harbouring them in me, I admit that their power exhilarated me, and I felt some solidarity with them – after all, they were part of me. So your disrespectful mocking offended me to the core. I was reminded of the fact that you'd betrayed my trust by sending me into the house of mirrors. You remained my sworn enemy.

My resentment towards you festered for the entire walk back, which I did gripping your arm, lids shut tight, I was so afraid of coming face to face with my reflection in some window as we'd turn a corner.

While you were busy bandaging, with an awkward gentleness, the cuts on my hand, I observed you through the frizzy fringe of my lashes. My anger intensified. I looked for a dent in your shields, a crack in your armour. I wanted to unseat you from your heroic pedestal, make you regurgitate your triumph, tear out your eyes whose composure provoked me.

I advanced on you at a frenetic pace, having lost control of my Perditions. Burning blood rushed to my lids, engorging them with intoxicating rage. My lacrimal caruncles pointed their turgescence at your eyes, and I shot a dark look at the very centre of your pupils.

You weren't expecting such an offensive and your eyelids struggled but I quickly overpowered you. Before you could have a chance to deploy the mercurial mirror of your shields, I ruthlessly tore apart your corneas, quartered the grooves of your irises, and pierced your crystalline lenses. Conquered, your pupils ceded to me, and I violated your abysses and battered your retinas without mercy.

This time, I didn't lower my lids when I climaxed. So I was able to see you close yours with the modesty of an ingénue. I withdrew, convinced that you were hiding something from me. And that, in the end, you were no stranger to shame.

My two Horrors must've slept that night, because I didn't see you get up. When I awoke, I was relieved to realize that I was alone in your lair and took advantage of your absence to put my thoughts in order. Nothing was keeping me here anymore: I had defeated you, Perseus – and I should now focus my attention on the benefactors.

I hadn't forgotten them during the thirteen days I'd spent with you. They owed me a rematch, and despite feeling some apprehension about returning to the institute, I was eager to challenge them at my own game and finally look them straight in the eye.

When you returned in the early afternoon, I didn't waste my breath asking you where you'd been; I wouldn't have believed one treacherous word of your explanations. What's more, you were shifty-eyed when you announced, "The benefactors have been told of your arrival. The time has come to go back to them."

I put on my glasses, and your clear eyes darkened: your guilty conscience weighed on your eyebrows. Would you have preferred that I struggle instead of obediently going to the slaughterhouse?

A mild spell had set in, and it was raining buckets. You had a fast car; the drive didn't take long. I couldn't help recalling the night my father had driven me to the lake, so long ago now. Then, I didn't know what awaited me. Now, I was prepared.

I asked you to let me out at the top of the driveway. I unlocked the door and was about to step out when you grabbed me by the hair.

"Wait a minute, I have a gift for you," you said, offering me a pendant.

I let you slip the chain around my neck and looked for a moment at the silver locket, its cover round and domed like a shield, adorned with golden gadroons. A pretty piece of jewellery you'd obviously stolen: the initials engraved on it had been chiselled off. I didn't thank you, because I was sure to regret it.

"There's a mirror inside," you said. "The day when you finally have the courage to look at yourself, I hope that you'll understand what I see in your eyes."

Want to know what I saw in yours in that moment? Kindness, solicitude, even tenderness. That's probably why I didn't throw the locket in your face. This sudden sentimentalism didn't move me, however. I got out of the car without saying goodbye and quickly walked away in the rain without turning around.

The old lake had not lost any of its gloom, nor the boarding school any of its sinisterness. At the end of its mooring line, the rowboat floated like a sarcophagus in the foetid water; the creaking door of the empty aviary banged in the wind. On this moonless, rainy night, even the light filtering through the windows seemed dull. Nevertheless, I looked on these familiar places with some emotion, because I was coming back with my head held high.

Twelve cars were lined up along the driveway: none of the benefactors was missing. They must already be waiting for me in the boardroom, while the protégées cooled their heels in the private wing. Evidently, the benefactors thought they were safe, since no dogs or matrons were picketing around the institute. Their assurance surprised me. Didn't they know what I was capable of?

Determined to destroy everything in my path, I put on my most murderous look and started up the stairs. Nothing could stand in my way. The doors opened, and the headmistress appeared on the threshold. As soon as I saw her large owl eyes, I understood that you'd betrayed me. That very morning, for a measly few dollars, you'd sold the secret of my vulnerability to the benefactors.

As a result, the headmistress was armed with glasses

that had two round mirrors for lenses and looked more menacing than cannons. Seeing my silhouette in their reflective surface, I didn't even have the instinct to make a run for it. I simply shut my lids and hid my face in my hands.

"We've missed you," the headmistress said in her venomous voice. "But here you are, back at last in your rightful place. And now that I know how to tame you, you'll never be able to escape me again."

With the tips of her nails, she pushed me into the aviary. I heard the grating of the door hinges, the clatter of a chain, the metallic click of a lock ... I had just enough strength to ask the headmistress if I would remain in this cage for a long time. She said, "You're too dangerous to be left free. The benefactors are deciding your fate as we speak. As soon as they've come to an agreement, I'll come back for you and bring you to them."

She left me in the pouring rain. I made sure that she'd definitely left with her mirrors of misfortune before I tackled the lock. Nothing to be done: it was solid, and the chains were indestructible. A blade of anguish cut my legs, and I collapsed in a pool of mud.

Because of you, I was at the mercy of the benefactors and in danger. What new maliciousness were these villainous men going to invent for me? Would they spread my lids wide and force me to look into a mirror? Or excise my ocular globes? And once they were done having their fun, would they keep me for their next visits or get rid of me by pitching me to the bottom of the lake, ankles and wrists tied, so that I'd end up as food

·

for the medusae? Either way, I thought my chances were slim and could already glimpse my end.

On hands and knees in the muck, I gave into despair. The headmistress was right: I deserved to be locked up like a wild beast. I didn't want to die, but admitted that it was unjustifiable to prolong my existence and that the benefactors would do well to eliminate me. I had no intention, however, of giving them this pleasure: I meant to destroy myself in my own way and by my own means. If I hadn't been imprisoned, I would've thrown myself into the lake to drown with the medusae.

Some discordant notes and loud voices started coming from behind the institute's doors. Before the headmistress could reappear, I grabbed the only weapon I had: the locket that you'd given me. Undoing the clasp, I wondered if my Petrifiances would preserve their lethalness after my death, like the tentacles of medusae and the head of Medusa, with which Athena once adorned her shield ...

For you, I had a last thought but won't force myself here to rant about your venality in descriptive epithets. You had not cut off my head like in the myth, you'd done something much worse: you had castrated my only means of defence. For this, I couldn't forgive you.

I took one last big breath, opened the locket shaped like a shield, and prepared to die turned to stone.

At the end of our lives, we all find ourselves before a mirror in which we are forced to contemplate the naked truth. No one escapes this. It is the last judgment – and the only one that matters.

In the mirror sprayed by the rain, my Medusae emerged from the darkness and through their revelation, everything became clear. All at once, I understood why my mother had felt such shame for giving birth to me, why my sisters had become so averse to me, why my father had had a stroke. I understood the headmistress's revulsion, Suzanne's fleeing, and the terror of the men who saw me. And I finally understood what you meant by "eyes of a woman."

Because each of these eyes offered the startling spectacle of an open, moist vulva – but this you know better than anyone. The upper and lower lids, fleshy like the swollen folds of the labia, were bristled with thick lashes the texture of pubic hair. In the inner corner of the eye, the lacrimal caruncle shamelessly protruded like a clitoris out of its hood. At the centre of the sclera, which was not white but engorged with blood and the colour of raw flesh, the violet nymphae of the iris throbbed frantically, and the ostium of the pupil disgorged its arousal fluid with a suction motion.

I was pulled up into this vaginal fold, passed through the hymen of the crystalline lens and the mucus of the vitreous humour, crossed the ciliary cervix, and emerged in the uterine womb of the retinas. At the centre of the endometrial lining, the maculae – the yellowish areas where the visual cells are concentrated – observed me like two flashing pupils.

I knew this arbitrary and implacable look intimately: it belonged to the monster who had enslaved me all my life. I'm referring to shame of course – the shame of the body, of its intimate parts and physical defects.

Do you remember our conversation about original sin? You talked about the blessed amorality that ruled Paradise before the Biblical fall, suggesting that the forbidden fruit, which promised knowledge of good and evil, had in fact only taught us to be ashamed of our own nakedness.

But tell me, do we not still hide behind the miserable fig leaves of coiffures, attires, and face paints because we care about how others see us and how mirrors reflect us? This enslavement ensures our obedience to the norms, our dread of what people might say, our subservience to the ideals of beauty, our submission to conformity ... I for one think that we'd all be much happier if we were blind.

Full of noxious disdain and deleterious hate, my maculae were, in a sense, my stain of original sin – the stigmata of my damnation. And now they sought to annihilate my amour-propre by painfully reminding me of all the denigration endured, the rejection suffered, the caresses rebuffed, the smiles not returned ...

The monster of shame didn't intimidate me. What did its opinion matter to me anymore? Now that I'd seen the beauty of my eyes, I was hardened against its murderous arrows. Like a mirror, I reflected back its own hideousness and with an exterminating look, heavy with all the suppressed feelings, unspoken words, unshed tears, and anger lurking deep in my soul, I petrified it. I reduced the maculae to two ovarian follicles that shimmered with the adularescence of moonstone.

I closed your locket. The mirror, after all, had not killed me. However, when I raised my eyes, I didn't recognize the lake or the forest because my vision had been transfigured. You could say that I'd acquired a third eye with which I could see the thrust of the vital force, its structure, its infinite forms, its ovulations, its budding, its incubations, its hatching, its proliferations, its copulations, its germinations ...

I saw sparkles in the water's depths, rhizomatic phosphorescences beneath the soil, and glimmers on the cattails. Before my eyes, the dazzling arborescence of sap rose along the trunks of fir trees and spread throughout the branches, illuminating them all the way to the buds. I perceived the nocturnal exhalation of the marsh plants, the obstinate swarming of underground insects, the beating of birds' hearts ... and of course the abundant pulsations of the medusae.

Life, glorious in all its uniqueness and all its imperfections, also flowed through me and instilled the same instinct in me, claiming my right to existence. Life pawed the ground like a spirited Pegasus, the winged horse that sprang from Medusa after Perseus cut off her head.

My eyes were not unnatural aberrations. If they

shocked, it was because of their animality, their immodesty, their disobedience. Like pagan gods, they echoed the archaic forces at the origin of creation ...

I was now ready to declare: I was Medusa. The eternal feminine. The manifestation of primordial chaos. The destroyer of all the world's mirrors. I had nothing left to fear – neither reflections nor shadows.

It was past midnight when the headmistress finally released me from the aviary. Once skeletal, she had become spectral and floated in her toga. She wore her owl, summarily stuffed, on her wrist. The rain streaked down over her shiny cranium and flowed in runnels over a face that the past year hadn't spared.

"Our dear benefactors are waiting for you with impatience," she said adjusting the mirrors on the bridge of her nose. "To mark your return among us, they have prepared a surprise for you that will certainly be remembered in the annals of the Athenaeum."

"What sort of surprise?"

"A big game, clearly. What else?"

She pulled me by the sleeve up the front steps. I kept my head down but could see through the bangs of my hair the entrance hall lit by lanterns and decorated for a child's birthday party, with dozens of balloons and brightly coloured crepe paper streamers. A cake decked with candles was set on a table, next to a pitcher of lemonade.

The benefactors were all wearing protective glasses like the headmistress. With their shirttails untucked and their party hats crooked, they capered about blowing kazoos. I know that it's hard to imagine, but they behaved even worse as a group than individually. Our national poet was playing the clown, perched on a stool. The governor had two fingers stuck in the cake's icing. The judge and zookeeper were throwing streamers at each other, shoving and pulling each other like little scamps.

As soon as they saw me, these gentlemen rushed to greet me with cries of joy, some giggling and elbowing each other, others coming up to pinch my cheeks. They told me the program of the night games, whose prime role they'd reserved for me: the judge of a belching contest, the treasure of a treasure hunt, the sheep of a jumping tournament, the seat of musical chairs, the hand of a clapping game, the donkey on which to pin the tail ...

Believing themselves safe behind their mirrors, they bragged and boasted and stuck their tongues out at me as though they were defying death. Soon, they started goading each other as to who could make the ugliest grimace – and I assure you, the competition was ferocious.

I observed their contorted expressions through my hair. The structure of the epidermis seemed magnified as though under a microscope. My crystalline lenses, which had the vergence of optical lenses, could discern the starry striations of the papilla, the overlapping of the pavement epithelium, the desquamation of the skin, the pigmentation of liver spots and red blotches ... By further contracting the ciliary muscles, I could even penetrate the crypts of the pores and follicles, all the way to the nerve endings and capillaries.

The life that flowed through these veins had lost its energy long ago. It was now unnatural, corrupted beyond all salvation. I could have, in that moment, put an end to the benefactors with one blink of an eye. However, that wasn't my intention. I confess, I wanted to toy with them a bit. And this time, I would amuse myself at their expense.

I could easily see their eyes through their glasses, and they were all converging on me. So I raised my head and let them get only a small glimpse of my half-closed eyes ... not enough to kill them. Just enough to Medusify them.

They stood there paralyzed, without really understanding what was happening, while I froze for all eternity, on their sileni faces, the distortions of their character vices. The wrinkled brow of narrow-mindedness. The flattened ears of indiscretion. The scowling eyebrows of intolerance. The drooping eyelids of laziness. The cross-eyes of egotism. The sly, dark circles of dishonesty. The liver-spotted nose of rudeness. The bloated cheeks of conceit. The contorted jaws of cruelty. The violet lips of meanness. The inane smile of infantilism. The lolling tongue of lechery.

The benefactors looked at each other, at first amused to see their grotesque faces. But their laughter faded once they tried in vain to relax their muscles and realized that their grimaces were permanent. They had become the monsters, and they would never again dare to show their faces in the society in which they had shone for so long.

As for me, my head felt light, my diaphragm joyful, my heart tickled by the blood sparkling in my eyes. I'd finally found an amusement worthy of my interest.

"I have a new game to propose to you," I told the benefactors. "Now, try to be taken seriously!"

They didn't accept my challenge. They bolted and fled into the night as fast as their feet could carry them.

The first thing I did after I freed the protégées was to open wide the doors to the library. They rushed to the bookshelves, raiding the stacks, and I saw life spark in them as though they were fireflies. The books also flickered with their ethereal, fluid fire, which lit up the protégées' faces as soon as they opened the pages.

I feel the same current flow through my pen as I write these last lines to you. How could I hold a grudge against you now? Your betrayal was certainly not heroic, yet your intention to make me see myself was commendable. Without your locket, I'd still be struggling with shame. Every time I gaze at my eyes in it, I feel an immense pleasure that is every bit the equal of the pleasure you gave me. Please know that I've kept the locket and treasure it.

All around me, the protégées are reading silently in leather chairs, among scattered volumes that they never put back. They haven't set foot in the study hall since they've taken over the benefactors' wing. The other night, they threw all the toys out the windows and burned them in a huge, joyous bonfire. I think that Suzanne would've found the scene delightful.

The headmistress is no longer here to impose discipline. I believed her to have left with the benefactors, but it's also possible that she decided to remain here for all eternity, since we found the boat drifting in the middle of the lake. Don't count on me to check, with my own eyes, whether or not her corpse rests at the bottom. I look towards other horizons now.

One day, I too will join the medusae. But in the meantime, life calls to me and I want to see where its current will take me. I won't look back. I won't think of you or anyone else. I won't shed any tears. I have a heart of stone.

ACKNOWLEDGMENTS

My blind gratitude to all those who participated, whether knowingly or not, to the development of this novel: Catherine Leroux, Véronique Desjardins, Julie Robert, Antoine Tanguay and the entire Éditions Alto team, Jean-Claude Cloutier, Mathieu Langlois-Larivière, Gabrielle Martin, Suzanne Myre, Michèle Mayrand, Luc Giard, Étienne, Mathieu, and Mathilde Gamelin-Desjardins, as well as the ghosts of Serge and Winnie.

OANA AVASILICHIOAEI interweaves poetry, translation, sound, and photography to expand and trouble ideas of language, histories, polyphonic structures, and borders of listening. Her six collections of poetry hybrids include *Eight Track* (Talonbooks, 2019, finalist for the Governor General's Literary Award and A. M. Klein Prize for Poetry) and *Limbinal* (Talonbooks, 2015). She has translated eleven books of poetry and prose from French and Romanian, including Catherine Lalonde's *The Faerie Devouring* (Book*hug, 2018, Cole Foundation Prize for Translation), Bertrand Laverdure's *Readopolis* (Book*hug, 2017, Governor General's Literary Award for Translation), and Daniel Canty's *Wigrum* (Talonbooks, 2013).

MARTINE DESJARDINS was born in the Town of Mount Royal, Québec, in 1957, the second child of six. After receiving a master's degree in comparative literature, she worked as a rewriter, translator, and journalist for many magazines and was the long-time book reviewer for *L'actualité*, the major French-language current affairs magazine in Canada. Her first novel, *Le cercle de Clara*, was published in 1997. She received the Prix Ringuet for *L'évocation* and the Sunburst Award in 2013 for *Maleficium*, which was also shortlisted for the Governor General's Literary Award. She is also a two-time recipient of the Prix Jacques-Brossard de la science-fiction et du fantastique for *Maleficium* and *La chambre verte*. Desjardins currently lives in the Town of Mount Royal, on the street where she was born. In her free time, she plays chess against herself.